The Animal, the Vegetable, and John D Jones

Also by Betsy Byars

Novels

The Night Swimmers
   (Winner of the American Book Award)
After the Goat Man
The Cartoonist
The Cybil War
The 18th Emergency
Good-bye, Chicken Little
The House of Wings
The Midnight Fox
The Pinballs
The Summer of the Swans
   (Winner of the Newbery Award)
Trouble River
The TV Kid
The Winged Colt of Casa Mia

Picture Books

Go and Hush the Baby
   (Illustrated by Emily A. McCully)
The Lace Snail
   (Illustrated by Betsy Byars)

The Animal, the Vegetable, and John D Jones

BETSY BYARS

Illustrated by Ruth Sanderson

DELACORTE PRESS / NEW YORK

Published by
Delacorte Press
1 Dag Hammarskjold Plaza
New York, N.Y. 10017

Text copyright © 1982 by Betsy Byars

Illustrations copyright © 1982 by Dell Publishing Co., Inc.

Manufactured in the United States of America

First printing

Designed by Judith Neuman

Library of Congress Cataloging in Publication Data

Byars, Betsy Cromer.
  The animal, the vegetable, and John D Jones.

  Summary: Two sisters look upon a beach vacation
with their father, his woman friend, and her son, as two
weeks in the wrong place with the wrong people.
  [1. Interpersonal relations—Fiction.   2. Vacations—
Fiction]   I. Sanderson, Ruth, ill.   II. Title.
PZ7.B9836An   [Fic]   81-69665
ISBN 0-440-00122-6   AACR2
ISBN 0-440-00131-5 (lib. bdg.)

For Kristie Harby

Clara sat in the backseat of the Mercedes, staring out the window. In the front seat her father and sister had been having a discussion about television for twenty miles.

"Actors are such fools," her sister, Deanie, was saying. "They get in a TV series and then they get the idea that they're big superstars and go off the show, and you never hear of them again."

"Like who, Deanie?" her father said.

"Well . . . like . . ." Deanie paused, then laughed. "See how forgotten they are? I can't remember a single name!"

Her father laughed too.

Clara leaned forward, stuck her head between the bucket seats, and said, "I'm planning a television show."

Deanie glanced around as if she were surprised to find Clara was still there.

"Are you, Clara?" her father said. "What's it about?"

Clara watched his face in the rearview mirror to see if he was interested. His eyes were on the road.

"It's a game show," she said abruptly.

"Just what the world needs," Deanie sighed. "Another game show."

"It'll be called . . ." Clara paused to think up a name and Deanie said, "Oh, I just thought of one—that doctor on *M*A*S*H*—McLean Stevenson."

Clara slapped her sister on the shoulder. "*I* was talking. You're not supposed to interrupt when other people are talking!"

"You were not *talking*. You were pausing to make something up. In pauses like that people are allowed to speak. Aren't they, Dad?"

"If they don't mind being hit. Go on about your TV show, Clara."

"If she's through making it up," Deanie said.

Clara drew back angrily. "It's called *Take Your Pick*," she said, "and on this show parents would have to pick their favorite child, and children would have to pick their favorite parent."

"That's a game show? Sounds like mass murder to me," her father said.

"Oh, I thought of another one," Deanie said. "Hoss on *Bonanza*."

"He died," her father said.

"Hoss is dead?"

"Yes."

"Well, that *is* depressing. I liked Hoss. I'm going to stop talking about this."

"Good," Clara said through her teeth.

The trips with their father, since the divorce, were always like this, with both of them trying to get his attention. And it wasn't fair, Clara thought. Deanie was two years older, two years smarter, two years funnier, and always managed to sit in the front seat.

Her eyes narrowed. She leaned forward. "Dad, if you had to go on a show like that—like *Take Your Pick*—which one of us would you say you liked best —me or Deanie?"

"Clara!" Deanie said in a shocked voice.

"I could never go on a game show," her father said calmly. He was a radio announcer, announced all the Chicago Bears games, and his voice was always under control.

"Why not? You'd be good," Deanie said.

"I could never look really happy about winning a microwave oven."

"I'm serious," Clara said. "I—"

"You're always serious— Oh, this is my favorite song," Deanie said, turning up the volume on the radio. "Don't you love the Bee Gees, Dad?"

"Not *that* much."

Deanie laughed. In the backseat Clara silently imitated the three notes of her sister's laugh.

"You know," Deanie went on, "everybody says we're all going to end up deaf—all the kids my age—from listening to loud music. Do you believe that?"

"What did you say?"

Deanie laughed again, the same three notes. Clara leaned back in her seat and snorted. If her mother had heard her, she would have said, "Don't make horse noises, Clara."

She stared out the window. When we get to the beach, Clara told herself, things will be different. At least I can swim better than Deanie. She imagined swimming with her father. "Come on, Clara," he'd call, and they'd dive through the breakers and swim for hours, while Deanie sulked alone on the beach.

Actually, she admitted, I don't swim *that* much better. She sighed.

Deanie was adjusting the volume on the radio. "Now is that quiet enough? It sounds like we're listening to somebody's radio two miles away."

"That's the way I like to listen to music."

Clara wished she had stayed at home. At least that way she would have gotten a moment of attention. She thought of herself at the front door, face set, while her father begged, "Please, Clara, please. We won't have any fun without you."

He wouldn't have begged, she thought. She closed her eyes. He would have said, "Well, if you really don't want to come . . ." But her mother—now, her mother might have begged. Her mother was going on a two-week vacation of her own—"a business and pleasure trip" she called it—but Clara had seen the clothes she was taking, and they looked more like pleasure.

Idly she began poking the back of her sister's seat, something she knew Deanie could not stand. Deanie glanced around. "Clarrra!"

"What?"

"Quit it!"

"Quit what? That?" She got in one final poke.

"Oh, Dad," Deanie said, turning to her father. "Did I tell you Marcia and I went to a wax museum? It was so boring."

"I can imagine."

"The figures didn't *do* anything. Everybody just stood around saying, 'Don't they look real? Don't they look real?' "

"Well, did they look real?"

"No! Even the real people—the ticket lady and the attendants—didn't look real!" Deanie laughed.

Behind her Clara silently imitated the laugh, stuck out her tongue at her sister's bucket seat, and settled back for a long afternoon.

John D Jones, Jr., was packing his suitcase. The bottom layer was a thick slab of paperback books, comic books, paper, pencils, notebooks, electronic games—all the things he would take if he were going into solitary confinement.

"John D," his mother said from the doorway. She had been standing there watching him pack. "Don't take all those games and books. I told you, Sam's daughters will be there. We'll be doing things. We'll—"

"I do not intend to do anything with Sam's daughters." John D did not bother to look up.

"They are very nice girls."

"Quite possibly."

"John D —"

"I am going on this trip," he said calmly, staring down

at his folded clothes, "for one reason." He looked up at her. "Because I have to."

Through his thick glasses his pale eyes were blurred, enormous. He held up one hand. "However, I will be my usual perfect self. I will do nothing crude. I will cause you no embarrassment. My perfect behavior will quite possibly make Sam's daughters look like the Wicked Stepsisters." He smiled slightly. "Although obviously I hope it will never come to that—stepsisters, I mean."

"John D, Sam and I are friends, and that friendship means a great deal to me. If you would just give him a chance, give the girls a chance. Clara is going into the seventh grade too. You could—"

John D closed his suitcase. "Mom, I am not going to participate in this two-family vacation, and that's final."

"John D—"

"No."

In the past year John D had discovered his power over his mother. All he had to do was speak firmly and quietly and he got his way. He was amazed at how simple it was. All those years he had spent falling on the floor and kicking and screaming. All those humiliating, tiring temper tantrums had been wasted. His whining alone, he figured, had taken up countless hours of his valuable life.

He was planning to have a chapter in the book he was writing about his discovery. "Simple Ways to Get What You Want" he would call it. It would be written in his usual clear, distinctive style and would point out such things as how much more powerful you appear when you aren't whining, bawling, or blubbering. "A runny nose is particularly ineffective," he would tell his readers.

John D's mother stood in the doorway, watching him. Her look was regretful, as if she were a potter whose clay had hardened before she got it the way she wanted it. She closed her eyes, then opened them to the same scene.

John D relented somewhat. "However," he added, "if Sam's daughters speak to me or ask me questions, I'll answer."

"I'm sure they will be very grateful," his mother said. The sarcastic tone of her voice made John D glance at her sharply. She turned to go.

"However," he added quickly, already sorry he had yielded. His pale eyes were suddenly sharp, vengeful behind the thick glasses. "I will answer in sentences containing exactly five words."

John D was pleased with his decision. He liked to set difficult goals for himself. He had once answered all the questions on a science test in exactly ten words and gotten his usual A.

"I . . . better . . . get . . . in . . . practice," he said, carefully counting out his five words.

His mother drew in her breath. This was the kind of thing she found particularly irritating. "Could you just once in your life try to be nice," she asked, "as a special favor to me?"

"I cannot understand anyone *trying* to be nice," he said. "I pride myself on the fact that I have never *tried* to be nice in my whole life."

"I believe that."

"When people tell me to have a nice day, I look at them like this." He glanced at her with distaste. "I read about a woman in Chicago who attacked someone who told her to have a nice day. I understand that woman."

"I don't."

"Mom, what if it were a plot? Did you ever think of that?"

"I have not got time to listen to—"

"What if some outer-space creatures . . ." He warmed to the idea. He swallowed. His words came quicker. "What if some outer-space creatures took human form in order to make us all nice, to brainwash us into being nice! They would go around saying, 'Have a nice day. Have a nice day.' They'd take jobs at checkout counters and pizza parlors. 'Have a nice day. Have a nice day.' Until finally we'd all become these nice people having these nice days, and then they'd step in and take us over, round us up like cows."

John D loved ideas like this. He pushed his glasses up on his nose. "When that happens, Mom, you'll be glad that there's one un-nice person left in the world to rescue mankind—your son."

"Oh, I imagine there'll be more than just you."

"Maybe not."

He stared beyond his mother, seeing himself as absolutely unique. He would be part of future history tests in schools.

34) Who was the last un-nice person on earth?

The thought of millions of children carefully writing in "John D Jones" pleased him. "Well, I know I got number thirty-four right," they would say later at recess, "because that is John D Jones!" He felt a flush of pride in his refusal to conform.

His mother was watching him. She said, "I never know when you're being serious."

"I'm always serious." He looked up at her with his pale eyes.

"No, you aren't, but you are very good at not letting people know when you are and when you aren't."

"Thank you."

"That wasn't a compliment, John D. You—" She sighed suddenly, as if she were letting off steam. "Well, I'd better finish packing." She pulled away from the doorway where she had been leaning. "We'll have to leave for the airport in a half hour."

"I'll be ready," he said. Then, remembering the five-word limitation he had put on his sentences, changed it to "I will be ready then."

His mother let out a muffled scream as she started down the hall. John D was, again, pleased. He liked the thought of himself as an antidote to the world's new niceness. He saw the world as a great big bland glass of niceness, and he was an acid tablet, dropped in to start things fizzing.

He snapped the latch on his suitcase and smiled.

Deanie, Clara, and their father were having supper in Howard Johnson's. Clara had ordered fried scallops, and her father was saying, "You ought to wait till we get to the island to order seafood."

"She likes tacky seafood," Deanie said as she politely cut her steak into small pieces.

"I do not."

"You do too. All you like is the fried batter. You don't even care what's inside."

"I do too!"

Deanie turned in her chair. "Anyway, you know what I heard, Dad? I heard you don't get real scallops anymore. It's too hard to catch real scallops, so you know what they do? They catch stingrays and cut out little round pieces with a cookie cutter. Marcia's father read that in a magazine."

"These are scallops," Clara said. "I can tell."

"Maybe," Deanie said, spearing a piece of steak with her fork. "Maybe not."

Clara stared down at her plate with sudden distaste. It was a known fact that she was bothered by food rumors. She had not bought a hamburger since the earthworm scare. She had stopped drinking bottled drinks the day a woman in Georgia found a mouse in one. She wouldn't eat hot dogs for fear of choking on rat hairs.

Suddenly it occurred to her that Deanie had probably tricked her into ordering the scallops in order to ruin her supper. She had really wanted a steak. It was Deanie who had said, "Oh, look, that woman's having scallops. They look delish. That's what I'm having."

Then, after Clara had ordered scallops too, Deanie had said, "Oh, I believe I'd rather have steak."

Clara looked up and caught her sister with a faint smile on her face. She strained to think of something that would ruin Deanie's supper.

Her eyes narrowed. She could cough on Deanie's steak if she could get close enough or, better still, sneeze on it, or at least knock her tea over. Her hand was sliding snakelike across the tablecloth toward Deanie's glass when her father spoke.

"Oh, by the way, girls," he said. His voice was casual,

no hint of trouble. "Did I mention that a friend of mine, Delores Jones, and her son, John D, will be sharing the beach house with us?"

Clara watched Deanie's expression go from smirk to shock in two seconds.

"What did you say?" Deanie's eyes blinked rapidly. This was a habit. She blinked every time she didn't understand something. Her teachers were always sending notes home suggesting she have her eyes checked.

"A friend of mine and her son will be sharing the house. I'm sure you've heard me mention Delores Jones. She and I have been seeing a lot of each other and, well, she and John D will be sharing the house."

Deanie put her fork and knife down beside her plate. She folded her napkin. It was as if she were trying to reverse the meal, to turn back the clock.

"Why are we sharing our house?" she asked, blinking three times.

Her father ran his hands through his hair. He was like a lot of radio announcers in that his looks did not match his deep voice. People who heard him announce the games were surprised to find he was tall and thin and didn't have much hair.

"Well," he said, "Delores had a vacation and was planning a trip to the beach, and we were planning a trip to the beach, and it just seemed sensible to share expenses. The house has four bedrooms—it's ridiculous to have them empty."

Deanie said, "Is it?" Her voice had the sharp click of a key in a lock.

"And you'll like Delores. She's very good company, very bright, very funny. She writes a kind of Dear Abby column for the Chicago paper. It's going into syndication soon."

"Dear Delores," Deanie said in a flat voice.

"Exactly!" Her father looked pleased. He began to cut his steak with renewed enjoyment.

"Does Mom know?" Deanie asked.

"What?"

"Does Mom know that this woman and her son are going along on our vacation?"

He looked thoughtful. "I don't know whether I mentioned it to her or not. It all came up kind of suddenly."

"I see."

Clara had been watching Deanie, enjoying her distress. Then, suddenly, the realization hit. A strange woman and her son were going to be sharing their vacation, their beach house, their father.

Her expression changed. Her lips tightened. Her cheeks puffed with distress— "frog cheeks," her mom called them.

"Clara, don't blow up like a frog every time something goes wrong," her mother would say.

"I don't."

"Well, you probably don't realize it—we all have little habits and mannerisms that we aren't aware of, little things—oh, what I would call animal behavior."

Now for the first time Clara was aware of her puffed cheeks. She drew in a breath, looked down.

Abruptly she pushed her plate away. "These scallops do taste funny," she said. "I don't think they are real."

The scallops rolled around her plate. She looked at the quivering scallops as disappointed as a woman discovering fake pearls.

"I told you so," Deanie said. There was no pleasure in her voice at all.

The two girls looked at each other. Their eyes, the soft brown eyes of their mother, shifted to look at their father. He was signaling the waiter for another glass of wine.

Deanie pushed her plate away too. "This doesn't taste like real steak either," she said. This time when she blinked her eyes it was to hold back her tears.

18

Deanie could not sleep. The lights flickering on the ceiling of the motel room, the happy shouts from the swimming pool—"Mom, watch this! Look at me!"— only made her feel worse.

She turned over in bed, pulling the sheet with her. She sighed aloud.

Her usual nighttime fantasy—that John Travolta was in love with her—would not work tonight. Even one of her favorite lines—"Dance with me, Deanie"— had a flat ring. It might as well have been spoken by, say, Bob Parotti from her homeroom.

"Will you lie still!" Clara hissed. "I'm trying to sleep." She lifted her head and frowned. In the thin light that filtered through the curtains her face looked as wrinkled as her pajamas.

"I can't help it. I'm restless." Deanie turned over again.

"Yeah, restless." Clara's tone implied there was much more to her sister's twisting and sighing than that.

Deanie glanced warningly at the other bed, where their father lay sprawled on the sheets in his pajamas. He was snoring softly.

"Anyway, I'm just as miserable about this as you are. I hate strangers." Clara flopped back on her pillow.

Deanie watched the ceiling. The two weeks with her father, which she had looked forward to all spring, were ruined. She had thought her only competition was Clara. She loved competing with Clara. All you had to do to upset Clara was to tell her, while she was eating Rice Krispies, that a woman had found a used Band-Aid in hers one time.

But Delores, flying in from Chicago, being very funny, very bright, great company, well, there wasn't going to be any pleasure in that competition. Deanie saw herself pushed into the background like one of the losers in a beauty pageant, wearing a bright frozen smile while inside seething with pain and disappointment.

She turned and wadded her pillow under her cheek. Outside, at the pool, someone cried, "Mom! Harold dropped my Barbie doll in the deep end!"

Good, Deanie muttered to herself.

"Mom, she had on her mink stole and formal!"

Even better.

"He's going to have to buy me another one!"

Deanie sighed again. She ran her fingers through her hair. She had planned to get up early, wash and blow-dry her hair, but now that seemed pointless. She wished she were at home. A new boy had moved into the apartment next to Marcia's, and Marcia had showed him Deanie's picture and he had said, "She's got sexy eyes." By the time she got home, he would have met somebody else. Anybody could have sexy eyes if they used the right makeup.

"Angh," she muttered beneath her breath.

"Did you say something?"

"No."

"Then be quiet."

She tried John Travolta again. It was no use. When her life was going well, so did her fantasies. She and John Travolta spun and dipped and twirled without a mistake. When her life went bad, Travolta became as clumsy and heavy-footed as Bull Durham in her school, who danced like he was making a tackle.

She turned one more time, easing onto her side so as not to disturb Clara.

When she was settled, she muttered, "And I gave up cheerleading camp for this."

"You did not *give up* cheerleading camp," Clara said, pouncing on the words like a cat. "Mom wouldn't let you go. She thinks cheerleaders are juvenile and stupid and sexist."

"She thinks that *now*. When she was a girl, she wanted to be a cheerleader like everybody else. She tried out and didn't get it."

"Mom never tried out for cheerleader."

Deanie went up on one elbow. "Aunt Flo told me. She said Mom cried when she didn't get it. Mom was first alternate, and she used to get down on her knees at night and pray that a regular would get sick."

"I don't believe you."

Deanie fell back on her pillow. "It's true. Mom thinks everything is sexist that she's too old to do. I think being a cheerleader is neat. And when I'm forty, I'm not going to—"

"Girls." Their father turned his face toward them. His head hovered over the pillow. "You have got to get some sleep."

"All right, but didn't Mom try out for cheerleader when she was in high school?"

"I didn't know her then," he said, falling back on his pillow. "We met in college."

Outside there was the sound of a splat on the pavement. "There's your old Barbie."

"She's ruined! Mom, Barbie's ruined."

Deanie sighed and closed her eyes. "I wish Barbie was the only thing that was ruined," she said to herself.

John D Jones, Jr., had never been bored in his life. This was because he had the constant companionship of the most intelligent, witty, and creative person in the world—himself.

To pass the time on the airplane, he was working on one of the chapters in his book. It was titled "You Are Smarter Than Your Teachers," and he was bent over his paper, making up the questions that would go at the end of the chapter.

1) If your teacher genuinely doesn't like you, you should
    (a) run to your parents and say, "Boo-hoo, my teacher doesn't like me."
    (b) blame your bad grades on the fact that your teacher hates you, say things like,

"Well, what did you expect? I told you she only gives A's to her pets!"

(c) say to yourself, "Many people will not like me in this world. That is their misfortune. I, who have better taste than they, like myself very much."

He was putting a period at the end of this sentence when the stewardess touched his shoulder. He looked up at her, startled.

"Would you like one of our inflight coloring books?" she asked.

"No." He gave her an expressionless look. He folded the corner of his paper over his writing so she couldn't read it.

"Are you writing a little story?" she asked, smiling, leaning closer.

"No."

He resisted the temptation to tell her he was writing quite possibly the most important and influential book of the century, a book that would change children and their lives forever.

The stewardess hesitated, then moved on down the aisle, looking for someone else to assist.

John D waited for his mother to say "The stewardess was just trying to be nice," but she was talking to the man beside her.

"Tell me about Pipe Island," she was saying. "This is my first visit, and I don't want to miss anything."

"Well, let's see. Its shaped like one of those long Indian pipes—that's how it got its name. Creek Indians lived there. The boy'll be interested in that."

John D kept writing.

"Up at the harbor end, my sister tells me, they've got a mall now and a McDonald's, condominiums, marinas. They filled in the marsh and made an eighteen-hole golf course."

"That does not sound like progress." His mother smiled. "I was looking forward to an *island*." She drew an isolated circle of land in the air with her hands. "You know, remote. . . ."

"Where will you be staying?"

"In a house. My friend who made the arrangements said it's down at the end of the island."

"You won't have to worry about condominiums down there. You won't be bothered except by fishermen."

"That's good to hear."

She began to move objects around in her purse. She pulled out her lipstick.

"Oh, one thing, ma'am. There's been a powerful current running off Pipe Island this year. If you do any swimming, you'd better watch out for it."

"What kind of a current? I know absolutely nothing

about the ocean." She smiled. "Except that I don't want to swim in it."

"Well, as my sister tells it, you're all right in the shallow water, but if you go beyond the swells, well, it'll take you right on out. Three people already drowned this summer, my sister said."

"But that's terrible."

"They were all people like yourself, ma'am, tourists who think the ocean's nothing but a big swimming pool. If you could see what-all's under there, you wouldn't go in over your knees."

"Did you hear that, John D?" his mother asked, turning to him.

He put a period at the end of his sentence and circled it. That was a sign to himself that this sentence was perfect and should never be changed.

"I don't plan on doing any swimming," he reminded her without looking up. "It doesn't affect me."

"Yes, but Sam's daughters will probably be swimming. They should be warned."

He looked up at her. She had paused with her lipstick just below her lips.

"Yes, they probably should be. That can be your first motherly duty."

"John D—"

"Ladies and gentlemen, we've begun our descent,"

the stewardess said over the loudspeaker. "Please extinguish all smoking materials and fasten your seat belts. Return your seat to its upright position . . ."

John D's mother quickly moved the lipstick over her lips and dropped it into her purse. The plane was just breaking through the clouds, and she looked out the window at the ocean.

"Beautiful!" she said. "Look, John D, there's the island and it *is* shaped like a pipe. Look, John D, we're staying way down at the end. It *is* remote."

The man touched his mother's arm. "When the wind comes from the north," he said, "that's usually when the currents run strong. Everybody that's been drowned was drowned when the wind came from the north."

The way he said it made John D think of a disaster movie made cheaply for TV. *When the wind comes from the north, someone will be pulled beneath the murky waters! Who will be the tide's next victim? Tune in Thursday night at nine for—*

"It's been nice talking to you, ma'am. I hope you and the boy have a real nice vacation."

"Thank you."

"**F**leas!" Clara yelled. "See, there *are* fleas in this house. I *told* you."

"There are no fleas," Deanie said.

"Well, what is that? Right there on my leg. Look! What is that?"

"Dirt."

"Does dirt jump?"

"Yours probably does."

"I'm telling you, there are fleas on me."

"Well, go buy yourself some flea collars, one for each ankle."

"That is not funny."

Deanie was practicing cheerleading routines in the living room of the beach house. Clara was sitting at the table, examining her legs. Their father had driven to the airport to pick up Delores and John D.

Deanie did not glance in Clara's direction. "Gimme a W!" she begged the rattan sofa. "Gimme an O!" she asked the open window. "Gimme an L," she turned to ask the kitchen.

"That is a *flea*," Clara said, bending over her leg.

"Gimme a V," Deanie went on. "Gimme an E! Gimme an S! Yayyyy, Woooooolves!" She leaped into the air, arms over her head, legs apart, and then landed heavily on the wooden floor.

Clara was looking at her fingers. The flea had been caught and was now trapped between Clara's thumb and forefinger. Clara made sure it was there, and then looked up at her sister. She watched her critically.

Deanie was now leaping into the air to celebrate an imaginary touchdown. "Yay, Wo-oo-oo-oolves!" she yelled. She did the word *wolves* as if she were howling. She loved that. It gave her goose bumps when everybody in the stadium did it. It was the best thing about getting a touchdown.

"You're not going to get it for cheerleader," Clara predicted flatly. She was holding her flea in her lap as if she were drinking tea.

Deanie turned, fists against her chest, ready for the next cheer. "How do you know? You're not even in my school."

"You're not the type."

"I'm as much the type as Cindy Annetto."

"No, you aren't. Anyway, nobody with skinny legs ever gets to be cheerleader, and you've got skinny legs."

"I do not."

Chin up defiantly, Deanie turned and went back to her cheers. "We got the team, yeah, team," she chanted. "We got the pep, yeah, pep. We got the—"

"You got the flea, yeah, flea!" Clara interrupted. She opened her fingers and threw the flea in Deanie's direction as if she were bowling.

Deanie stopped abruptly. She turned. She walked slowly toward Clara. "Now, just what did you do that for?"

"Because I felt like it."

"You *felt* like throwing *fleas* on people? You're sick, you know that? You need to see a head doctor."

"If anybody in this family needs a head doctor, it's you!" Clara said.

"I'm not the one who's throwing *fleas* at people."

"Well, I'm not the one who kisses herself in the mirror and gets lipstick all over the glass!"

"Clara!" Deanie drew in her breath. "Clarrrrra!"

"And," Clara went on with the confidence of someone who is hitting the mark, "I don't use a mouthwash that makes me 'Kissy clean' and I don't use deodorant that makes me 'close-up fresh' and I don't—"

"No, you don't wear deodorant at all. That's why you smell like a horse—and to complete the picture, you also snort like a horse."

"I do not!"

"And you grunt like a pig and screech like an owl and pick fleas off yourself like an orangutan."

"Well, you wear Missy Maiden bras that give you that 'little bit extra' when what you need is a whole lot extra!"

"Animal!" Deanie yelled.

"Vegetable!"

"Nyaaah!"

"Nyaaah!"

They stuck their tongues out at each other with satisfaction. Each felt she had hit the target, summed up the other's weaknesses. It was worth it—even having to hear her own faults—to at last expose the other's.

Suddenly Deanie straightened. She looked at the door. She had planned, when her father arrived with Delores, either to be reading something intelligent, smiling to herself—or writing a letter, smiling to herself. Now, unconsciously, her lips drew back in a half smile.

"What is wrong?" Clara asked, irritation showing in her face and voice.

Deanie nodded toward the doorway.

"If you are trying to make me think that there's somebody in the doorway," Clara said, "if you are trying to make me think that Dear Delores and her cretin son have arrived and are—"

Something in Deanie's face made her break off. She turned.

In the doorway stood a black-haired woman and, beside her, a boy who was obviously her son. The woman had the remains of a smile on her face. She lifted one hand and took off her dark glasses. The boy's glasses were so thick, his eyes looked like reflections in a pool.

"Well, did you all introduce yourselves?" The girls' father appeared on the porch. He edged into the room and set the suitcases down. Then he looked around at the silent four, his smile growing puzzled.

"Well?" He looked from one to the other. "Did you meet?"

Delores came to her senses first. She stepped forward, really smiling now. "No, but I know that you must be Clara, and you're Deanie." She came forward and let one hand rest on each of the girls' shoulders.

"Yes," said Deanie. Her face was as red as if she'd been in the sun all morning instead of practicing her cheerleading routines in the house.

Clara drew in one long shuddering breath that ended in a whinny. "Yes," she said.

33

She and Deanie both began watching the floor intently. Clara felt as if she could never look up again.

"John D," Delores went on cheerfully, "these are Sam's daughters, Deanie and Clara." She tapped the girls' shoulders lightly.

"Yes, I've got them straight," John D said from the doorway.

There was an amused tone to his voice, and each girl felt he was adding to himself, "Deanie is the Vegetable and Clara is the Animal."

He stepped forward and stopped when his tennis shoes were in their line of vision. In the same amused voice he added, "They're just as I imagined."

Clara shuddered. She felt Delores's hands tighten, then give three quick comforting pats.

Clara kept looking down at her feet. There was a flea on her ankle. Probably the same one, she thought. He had hopped all around the room after she'd thrown him away. "Where'd the Animal go? Where's the Animal?" And now, finally, "Here she is," and on he hopped.

She was too miserable to scrape him off. The misery was pumping through her body now, like blood, going to every cell.

"So what do you think, John D?" she heard her father say in his man-to-man voice.

"Everything's about as I expected," she heard John D answer.

"And," Delores said, giving the girls a final hug, "we're all going to be great friends."

Deanie and Clara came over the dunes, rattling the sea oats as they walked. They slipped down the soft sand without speaking, crossed a strip of shells and shards as hard as pavement, and started up the beach.

"Do you think they heard us?" Clara asked then, glancing at her sister.

"Of course, they heard us," Deanie snapped back. She yanked her bathing suit top up by the straps and pulled the bottom down in the back. She had been in such a hurry to get out of the house that she had not bothered to cover herself with her usual layer of tanning butter.

"Maybe they didn't," Clara said. "Maybe—"

"Did you see the looks on their faces?"

"I had my head down most of the time."

"Well, I saw them and, believe me, they heard us."

They walked on in silence. The waves were gentle. The sand bubbled with the shifting of the sand fleas. Ahead of them the sandpipers ran up and down the shoreline, staying just ahead of the breaking waves.

"I hate him," Clara said abruptly.

"I hate both of them."

"Well, I do, too, but I hate him the most. You know who he reminds me of?"

"Who?"

"Remember that movie we saw with that real creepy kid who had been possessed by the devil and he would go around with this innocent little smile while his eyes were causing wrecks and setting people on fire? That's who he reminds me of."

"I agree. There's something wrong with that kid."

"And he probably thinks there's something wrong with us!" Her voice broke at the unfairness of it.

Deanie moved to the water and began to march through the shallow waves. She kicked her feet and sent water spraying ahead of her.

Clara watched. She was bigger than her sister and clumsier.

She was actually beginning to feel like an animal, she decided. The best she could hope for in life was to be

trained. With training she could lumber through life like a circus bear, upright and obedient, waiting to plop down on all fours when nobody was looking.

"I have just one goal for these two weeks," Deanie said, taking out her fury on the water, kicking like a football player. White foam flew into the air and blew along the hard sand.

"What?"

"To get a really good tan and gain ten pounds. I mean, that is the absolute most I can hope for now. A good time is out of the question."

"I also have one goal."

"What?"

"To make that stupid John D as miserable as he's made me."

"Put some sand fleas in his bed," Deanie suggested. She smiled slightly. "And while you're at it, put some crabs in hers. That would be appropriate." She stopped. "You know what? I just figured something out. Here's what's wrong with the world. Things happen to the wrong people. It's as simple as that. I mean, the wrong people get caught looking stupid and the wrong people get it for cheerleader and the wrong people get divorced." She paused. "Look, there are people—Betty Higgin's parents, for example—well, it would be all right if they got divorced. They fight all the time, right in front of Betty's friends. He locked her mother out of the house during Betty's slumber party. Did I tell you that?"

"Yes."

"Only who gets a divorce? Our parents, who never fight, never quarrel, never embarrass us."

"Just want to go their separate ways."

"I hate that expression. Anyway, it would be fine if Delores and her son had got caught looking stupid. I wouldn't have minded that at all. Only it was us! Oh, let's sit down. My legs hurt. When you don't have any muscles in your legs . . ." She trailed off.

"You have muscles."

"Tiny ones." Deanie flopped down on the sand, dug holes for her heels, and stretched out her legs. "If each of my legs weighed a half pound more, I would be happy with myself."

"You can have a pound off the tops of mine. I've got dinosaur legs."

"Wouldn't that be great?" Deanie said, sitting up straighter. "I mean, what if you could just go out and grab some pounds off of somebody? Here, I want some of your fat!" she said. She pretended to grab a pound from an imaginary person and deposited it on her legs, smoothing it out with a wave of her hand. "There, perfect."

"But then real fat people would always be trying to slap pounds on *you*," Clara said.

"I never thought of that." Deanie grinned. "And you wouldn't dare get near a fat person in an elevator because pow-pow-pow, and by the time you got to the fourth floor, you'd be covered with excess fat!"

She imitated a startled person reeling out of the elevator, looking down in amazement at the new flab. "And they'd be in such a hurry to get rid of it that they'd slap it anywhere! Probably on your head!" She puffed out one cheek and eyed it with horror.

Clara's smile brightened then faded. Her sister's funniness, her small hands fluttering over the deposits of imaginary fat, the comic look in her eyes—it all made Clara feel clumsier than ever.

"I don't want to go back to the house." She dug her heels into the sand as fiercely as if she were digging a foundation.

"Who does? Anyway, did you get a good look at her?"

"No."

"Well, she is the exact opposite of Mom. Mom has short grayish hair and Delores has black hair pulled straight back. And Mom's clothes—well, you know how she wears those handmade necklaces with beads and feathers, and embroidered peasant blouses, and Delores — Did you at least notice what she had on?"

"No."

"A perfect suit and a perfect blouse."

"It figures."

"I wish I could call Mom. 'Hi, Mom, I just wanted to tell you that Clara and I are doing fine and aren't getting too much sun or swimming out too far and don't worry about us, because Dad's girl friend Delores is here to look after us.' "

"She would say, 'That's nice. Remind Clara not to snort.' "

"Oh, Clara." Deanie got to her feet and brushed the sand off her legs. "Enough of this." She adjusted her bathing suit—up in front, down in back. "Let's go."

Clara stared at her. How could anybody, embarrassed as they had been, shake like a wet dog and jump right back into the water?

"You're going back to the house?"

"Yes, I'm hungry. I've set a goal for myself—three peanut butter sandwiches between meals."

Clara squinted at Deanie. "You *want* to go back," she accused. She put one hand over her eyes to block out the sun. She wanted to see her sister's expression. "You *do* want to go back."

"I don't *want* to go," Deanie said calmly. She flexed her arms in a quick cheerleading movement. "It's just that we have to go back sometime. Besides, I want to see what's going on."

"I'm never going back."

"Clara—"

Clara folded her arms around her legs and leaned over her knees. Her brown eyes watched the sea with the intensity of a sailor.

"Listen, the longer we stay out here, the stupider we're going to look. Now, come on, let's go in and act like nothing happened." Deanie started up the beach and then glanced back at Clara. "Come on!"

Clara got to her feet. She sighed heavily. The sun was hot on her head. The part in her hair, she thought gloomily, would probably be sunburned in the morning, would peel, and look like dandruff.

She watched her sister. Deanie was bouncing along the beach like somebody in a shampoo commercial.

The main difference between people, Clara decided as she stood there, was what they did after they stumbled and fell. They either bounced right back up like rubber, undented, unmarked, or they sat there and wondered if they would ever move again.

She herself fell into the sit-there division. Her body didn't want to do anything. Idly she poked some sand into a crabhole with her toe.

43

"Will you come on?" Deanie called. She turned, holding her long thick hair back in a ponytail to keep it out of her face.

Dragging her feet through the soft warm sand, Clara followed.

John D had not written a word in his book since his arrival at the beach house.

Coming into the house and finding the girls screaming insults at each other, perfect insults—insults that told him everything he wanted to know about them—well, it had been like the opening of a play. No, it was better than a play. It was like one of those TV shows that presents its most exciting scene before the first commercial to make people watch the rest of the program. If he had written the dialogue himself—he admitted this—he could not have made it better.

He was standing at the window, watching for the girls, when he saw them coming up the beach. He wanted to jump up and down like a child at Christmas who spies gift-laden grandparents. "They're coming!" he almost yelled to the empty house.

More rudeness, he thought happily. He rubbed his hands like an evil spirit. More insults. More of the awfulness that makes life worthwhile. ˙

They live in human bodies, but lurking beneath the flesh and muscle are—dah-daaaaaah!—the Animal and the Vegetable! Coming soon to your local theater or drive-in.

He smiled. He had not had this much pleasure since he had caught his English teacher in a series of grammatical errors.

Exiled from their planet, this unspeakable duo destroys anything that breathes or grows. Starring in their original roles are—dah-daaaaaah!—the Animal and the Vegetable! Also appearing nightly, in person, at Pipe Island.

He stepped closer to the window. He noticed that Deanie, the Vegetable, was walking in front, head up, one hand holding her hair, one hand pulling her bathing suit down in back.

The Animal was walking behind her, slowly, head down, hands dangling at her sides, as reluctant—let's face it, John D decided—as a mule.

He watched them without blinking. Then, as soon as he saw them start over the dunes, he crossed the room, flopped down on the sofa, and picked up a magazine. He pretended to look at an advertisement for lingerie.

He heard the screen door open. It would be Deanie, he knew, waiting on the porch, holding the door for Clara. "Come on," she said impatiently.

Yes, come on, John D urged.

"No!"

Clara remained—John D could picture it—with her legs planted in the sand.

Deanie said, "Listen, the car's gone, so they're all at the grocery store. You heard them say they were going."

He heard the faint sound of Clara's answer. She was probably saying, he decided, that she didn't want to come in the house even if no one *was* there. She never wanted to come in the house again as long as she lived. He loved it when he knew exactly what people were saying.

He drew in a breath of anticipation and licked his lips. It was Deanie who interested him at the moment.

She didn't disappoint him. "Come on," she said. Her voice was rising with excitement. "Listen, Clara, this will give us a chance to snoop in their suitcases!"

"Oh, all right."

He heard her start up the stairs and clomp across the porch.

"You take his," Deanie said. "I'll take hers."

"All right."

Clara came through the living room door first. "Deanieeee," she bawled as she caught sight of John D on the sofa.

"What is it now?"

Deanie came in, pulling at her bathing suit. She paused as she saw John D reading his magazine. He held the magazine up slightly so that they could not see that he had been looking at an advertisement for lingerie.

Deanie clapped one hand over her mouth. John D took her gesture as one of horror, the gesture of a person who has said something so terrible, that even now, too late, she is trying to seal her mouth shut.

He smiled to himself. If he had planned it, he couldn't have made it more perfect. He watched her, careful to keep his pleasure in her distress hidden.

Then abruptly his pleasure began to fade. Deanie's shoulders were shaking. Her eyes met his and squeezed shut with laughter.

John D straightened on the sofa. A small frown pulled his eyebrows together.

With her hand over her mouth Deanie ran from the room. She ran like someone who was going to be sick, but instead of going into the bathroom, she went into her bedroom and flopped across the bed. Then the

48

sounds of her helpless laughter, smothered in the covers, came to him.

John D let his magazine drop down into his lap. He looked at Clara.

Clara looked back. For a moment it was as if they were playing a game to see who would blink first. Then Clara turned and left the room.

"What's so funny?" she asked her sister.

In the bedroom Deanie tried to speak, but she was laughing too hard. She buried her face in the spread. The bed rattled with her laughter.

"What is so funny?" Clara demanded. She herself was closer to tears than laughter. She wanted to shake her sister. Deanie did this all the time—laughed so long over some secret hilarity that Clara got red in the face waiting to hear it. Then, Clara thought, her face growing redder, then it turned out to be nothing—someone had mayonnaise on their chin or toilet paper stuck to their shoe.

"What is so funny?" she asked through clenched teeth.

"He—" Deanie was trying to speak now. "He—he—he—"

Her words had the sound of more laughter, but in the living room John D had the uncomfortable feeling she was beginning a sentence about him.

"He what?" Clara asked angrily.

Deanie finally got it out. "He—he—was reading *Modern Bride* magazine!"

Then she gave herself up to her laughter, no longer trying to smother it. She flipped over on her back, laughed up at the ceiling, whooped.

John D looked down at the magazine, at the bride on the cover. *Modern Bride* magazine. Six Steps to Becoming a More Beautiful Bride. Trousseau Tips. He felt a flush redden his cheeks. He had not even known what he was reading.

"There is nothing funny about that," John D commented.

The line of displeasure between his eyes deepened. His dark eyebrows touched. He let the magazine drop onto the floor, then kicked it under the sofa.

For the first time since he had arrived at the beach house, John D had spoken a sentence that did not contain exactly five words, and he was too angry to care. His pale eyes burned.

In the bedroom Clara's clear voice echoed John D's thoughts. "I really don't see anything funny about him reading a bride magazine."

"I do," Deanie said. Her laughter subsided. She wiped her eyes. "I mean, here he was, acting so superior —like this big intellectual, like he was Einstein and we were Heckle and Jeckle—and then the minute we're out of the house, he's poring over a bride magazine." Her laughter bubbled again.

"He'll hear you," Clara warned.

"Who cares? At least I got one good laugh out of the two weeks."

Deanie lay still for a moment, worn out from all her laughter, as limp as a child who had been tickled too much. Then she pulled herself up, went into the bathroom, and began to run water in the basin.

She inspected her face in the mirror, right side, left side. Over her shoulder she said, "Don't let me go out in the sun again without my tanning butter."

Clara sat down on the bed. She began rubbing her feet against each other to get the sand off. She heard John D mutter "Idiots" in the living room.

She glanced down at the dusting of sand on the floor beneath her feet. "This is going to be a miserable vacation," she said.

Deanie leaned out the bathroom door and grinned. "I don't know. I'm beginning to enjoy it."

hey were cooking hamburgers out on the beach, and Delores was laughing as she attempted to turn a patty with two small forks.

"Let me help," Sam said.

"You helped before. That's why all those burned hamburgers are down in the coals. If you help anymore, we'll have to go to McDonald's!" She laughed.

"It's like one of those old beach party movies," Deanie commented to Clara. "Our father and Delores are Frankie Avalon and Annette Funicello."

"I knew it seemed familiar."

Deanie and Clara were stretched out on a blanket. John D had brought out a folding armchair, and he was sitting like an old man looking out to sea.

John D felt apart, and he wanted everyone to know it. Each time Deanie and Clara laughed at something—

there, they just did it again. Each time they laughed, he felt a wave of anger wash over him. They knew this, he thought, sitting up straighter, and they were over there on the blanket actually planning their laughter. "Come on," Deanie was probably saying, "one . . . two . . . three—laugh!" He did not know when he had felt such dislike for two people.

"John D, are you ready for a hamburger?"

He looked at his mother. "Whenever you manage to get one cooked."

She didn't even hear him. She was laughing again. Possibly she had ruined another hamburger. What had gotten into the woman? he wondered. He made a silent vow never to fall in love.

He looked to the sea. He thought that if his mother had spent her entire life thinking up a way to make him miserable, she could not have been more successful. He felt like a wire that had suddenly lost its insulation.

He had always enjoyed his aloneness, his uniqueness, but tonight he felt just plain lonely. Suddenly he wished for the father he had never seen, the father who had died, as nearly as John D could figure out, a half hour before he was born.

He sighed, slumping lower in his chair.

And it wasn't just because, well, if his father were here, then Sam and his idiotic daughters wouldn't be.

It was more a feeling that he would actually enjoy his father's company this evening.

It was ironic that the one person in the world whose company he had ever wanted was—

"Here you go," his mother said cheerfully, handing him a hamburger. He lifted the top of the bun and was disappointed to see that she had cooked the hamburger exactly the way he liked.

He heard Deanie say to Clara, "Afterwards we'll probably sit around a campfire and sing. 'Te-lllll me why-yyyyy.'"

John D wished he didn't have such good hearing. He no longer wanted to hear what the girls were saying. He thought of moving his chair farther away, but that would be what his mother called antisocial.

"Don't count on me," Clara answered. "I'm going swimming again."

"Now, don't go out too far," Deanie said in his mother's voice. "I sat by this man on the airplane, and he said that his sister said that there was a terrible current that would—"

"Girls! You ready to eat?"

Deanie broke off her imitation to call cheerfully, "Yes, we're starved." She got up and pulled Clara to her feet.

"Anyway," she said, "I don't see how you can swim in the ocean—all that seaweed and stuff. It's like soup."

"I like it."

John D bit into his hamburger and chewed. The meat had been cooked perfectly, but it tasted like paper.

Once in school John D remembered his class had had to write themes on why they wanted to be adults. Kids wrote "so I can drive a car" and "so I can stay up all night" and "so I can have as many cats as I want," and he had written—he could remember it perfectly— he had written, "I want to be an adult so that I will not have to suffer the company of stupid people." An incredibly intelligent sentence for a second-grader. He still felt exactly the same way.

"You are *not* going to eat one of the burnt ones!" Sam was saying to his mother.

"I am perfectly happy with a burnt one. I like my meat well-done."

"You do not."

"I like hamburgers well-done."

"Take this one."

"No."

"Come on, take it."

His mother pulled back her hands just in time to let the good hamburger, the only one left, fall into the sand. His mother threw back her head and let out a peal of laughter that would have done credit to a hyena. John D glanced at Sam to see if he was as disgusted over the picture of a grown woman laughing at a ruined hamburger as he himself was.

No, Sam was laughing too. John D watched them with an expression of distaste.

"Hey, why don't we go in to that little seafood restaurant you wanted to try?" Sam said to Delores. "You kids wouldn't mind, would you?"

"No," John D said.

"Why should we mind?" said Deanie, swallowing a bite of her hamburger.

"We won't be long."

As they started toward the dunes Sam turned and said, "I noticed a Monopoly game in there on the book-case. You could play after you go in."

Deanie looked at Clara and let her eyes roll up into her head. Then she turned her face toward John D.

Possibly, he thought with alarm, she intended to share her amusement over the proposed game of Monopoly with him. He looked quickly out to sea, pretending to scan the horizon for a ship.

"You know what I just read somewhere?" Deanie said. Now that her father and Delores were over the dunes, she didn't bother to soften her voice. "I read that the seashore—it has something to do with the meeting of land and sea—is such a dynamic place that it makes passions run higher, emotions stronger. It's like a full moon to a werewolf." She laughed.

"I'm going swimming," Clara said abruptly.

John D got up too. He folded his chair, put it under his arm, and got to the house just as his mother and Sam drove away.

"I'm sort of looking forward to this," Deanie said. It was the next morning, and she was watching herself in the mirror as she blow-dried her hair.

"I'm not," Clara said.

"Remember when we were little and we'd go to Fun World, and they would have statues of Bugs Bunny and Elmer Fudd and Tweety Bird beside the rides, and if you weren't as big as Tweety, then you wouldn't get to go?"

Clara nodded. She was sitting on the bed, hands in her lap, shoulders sagging. She had spent a miserable night. She had tossed and turned for hours, trying to get to sleep. And when she did sleep at last, she dreamed she had vomited all over her blouse and when she tried to wipe it off, she got the vomit all over her hands, and then she wiped her hands on her skirt and on her face and arms and then—she was desperate now, because John D was coming—on her hair and on her sunglasses, and when John D arrived with that small knowing smile of his, she was standing there with her entire body covered with vomit.

Now, this morning, still feeling ill, she was faced with a living nightmare. They were all going to Seven Continents for a day of rides and fun, and the thought of sitting in the backseat next to John D made her shudder.

"Promise me I won't have to sit by John D," she asked Deanie for the third time.

"I used to get just desperate." Deanie went on as if Clara had not spoken. "I'd run up to every statue and stand there. 'Am I big enough? Am I big enough?'" She stuck out her tongue and panted like a puppy.

"I don't remember that."

"That's cause you *were* big enough," Deanie said, giving her hair a final flip.

"I've always been big enough."

"Anyway, the thing I remember most—the real blow —was that to go in Haunted City you had to be as big as Casper the Friendly Ghost—and I wasn't—and I cried so hard, my nose ran all over my ice cream."

"Girls, are you ready?"

"And believe me, snotty peach ice cream is—"

"Girls!" their father called louder. "What are you doing in there?"

"Nothing, Dad," Deanie called back cheerfully. "We're on our way."

"Promise me," Clara said. She got off the bed and crossed the room to Deanie.

"What?" Deanie asked. She was still admiring her hair. "Never get between me and the mirror," she said to Clara, laughing. "My hair only looks good at the beach for fifteen seconds. Then I start to look like Frankenstein's bride."

Clara shifted out of the way. "Promise!"

"What?" Deanie asked.

"That I won't have to sit by *him*." There was something about the thought of touching John D . . . "I just hate to sit by people who don't like me."

"Everybody feels that way."

"Not like me."

"Yes, like you. That's why I almost flunked math— because I had to sit by Marie Edwards, and we have hated each other since first grade. She would deliberately make mistakes so that when I copied off her paper I'd get them wrong."

"Promise, Deanie."

"Listen, I can't promise anything. I have no control

over these terrible two weeks whatsoever, or over these terrible people."

"You do! You can! Just promise to sit in the middle!"

Deanie turned away from the mirror, satisfied. She grinned. "I am a puppet in the hands of Fate." She wiggled her way comically to the door, ankles wobbling, arms flailing helplessly in the air as her strings were pulled from above.

"That's not funny," Clara called after her. "That's the way I really feel."

Slowly, arms dangling, shoulders drooping, she followed her sister into the living room.

John D had not slept well either. After supper a really troubling thought had hit him. At the first opportunity Deanie and Clara were going to snoop in his suitcase! They would have done it this afternoon if he hadn't been sitting there looking at a magazine.

With that thought he had felt himself writhing like a snail turned out of its shell. He had never before been concerned about his privacy. His mother believed parents should respect their children's property absolutely—she had written an entire column on it. But Deanie and Clara—they obviously respected nothing. He felt as if he had fallen into the hands of creatures no longer governed by human values.

As the night wore on he imagined the girls ruthlessly tearing through his suitcase, pulling out one article after another.

"Look at this!" Clara would cry. "Asthma pills!" She would whinny like a horse.

And Deanie—Deanie would be laughing so hard, she would not be able to speak. "He—he—he—" she would cry, waiting for the hilarity to let up. "He—he—he wears Fruit of the Loom underwear!"

Then he sat straight up in his bed, mouth open with shock. His manuscript. What a time they would have with that!

"Listen to this," Clara would cry. " 'A runny nose is particularly ineffective.' "

"He—he—he," Deanie would answer.

He put one hand to his forehead. The thought of his words, the words he had written with such care, the thought of those words being read aloud by idiots—it was more than he could bear.

And perhaps they would come across the notebook in which he was practicing his autograph. Twenty-seven pages of his name, written over and over, line after line, so that when he became famous, he would have a bold, distinctive signature instead of the tiny uninteresting name he put to his homework papers. They would never understand that.

He got out of bed, stood on the bare sandy floor, and looked around the moonlit room. It was a room without hiding places—a chest, two beds, a table, his suitcase. He could possibly hide his manuscript and notebook under the mattress, but that would be the first place they would look.

"Aha!" Clara would cry, pulling up the mattress like a playful gorilla, and Deanie would once again answer, "He—he—he."

He had stood a long time in the moonlight, as bothered as a prisoner trying to hide something in a bare cell. Then he had crawled back into bed and let out a sigh so long, it seemed to empty his body of air.

He lay without moving, his legs drawn up to his chest. A miserable knot of humanity, he stared at the wall like a sick person waiting for his medicine to start working. With the first light of dawn he had fallen into a troubled sleep of an hour and fifteen minutes.

Now it was morning. Miserable, suspicious, vengeful, and unrested, he followed his mother to the car.

"Here, hold this," she said cheerfully, handing him her purse. She tied a blue bandanna on her head, looking in the side-view mirror. "How are you getting along with Sam's daughters?"

"As expected."

"Did you play Monopoly last night?"

"Hardly."

"Now, John D, they are very nice girls." She put her dark glasses on top of her scarf and looked at him. "Especially Clara. I believe you two could—"

"They are hardly nice girls, Mom."

She hesitated. "Then," she said with a faint smile, "you should be getting along well. You told me the other day that you hate everything nice, so if they aren't nice, well, then you should enjoy their company."

"I have never admired or enjoyed stupidity," he said in the calm cool voice that always stopped her.

"John D—" He met her eyes without blinking. She hesitated, then pulled her dark glasses over her eyes. "At least let other people have a good time."

"I'm not stopping anybody."

"I *have* to sit by a window!" It was Clara. "I get carsick." She was coming down the steps behind Deanie and her father. Her face was red, her cheeks as puffed as an adder's.

"Here, here's your purse," John D said quickly. He thrust it at his mother before the girls could see it on his arm and go into another one of those explosions of laughter they were so famous for.

"How's it going this morning, John D?" Sam asked, and then said in a lower voice to Delores, "I've never seen that outfit before. I like you in blue."

66

He leaned forward. Delores smiled and fluttered her eyelashes like a lovesick cat in a cartoon.

John D turned away in disgust. He did this just in time to see Deanie turn to Clara, grinning and fluttering her eyelashes in a perfect imitation of his mother. Did she—he wondered suddenly—imitate him as well?

He drew in his breath, turned, tried to get in the car so quickly that he stumbled, fell, and struck his shin. Pain shot all the way up to his eyebrows. He knelt in the backseat, bent over, unable to move.

"We're not in *that* big a hurry," his mother said. Her laughter was low, amused. She leaned forward then and put one hand on his back. "I'm sorry. Did you hurt yourself?" Her voice was concerned now.

"No."

His face, turned away from his mother, was red, burning hot. His voice, when he managed to speak again, was cool.

"I fell," he went on, "in order to test the humor level of the group. As I suspected, it is low."

He got to his feet. "On a scale of one to ten, I rate the group as a two, the category for those who laugh at the world's misfortunates."

"No one laughed," his mother said uneasily.

John D sat and faced forward. Now, at last, I hate every single person present, he thought.

"Well, let's go," Sam said. He pressed the girls into the backseat, Deanie on one side of John D, Clara on the other.

The car started. Shells crunched beneath the tires. As they turned left out of the driveway John D bumped into Deanie's shoulder. As they turned right onto the road he touched Clara's. I'm going to be clanging back and forth between these idiots all the way to the amusement park, he thought. He closed his eyes.

Trapped between the Animal and the Vegetable, all lines of escape cut off, what will be the fate of the proud young hero? Who will survive? Tune in—

For once he failed to amuse himself.

Twenty miles down the road, when they were driving over the causeway, one of a long line of cars and campers and trailered boats, with his mother reading aloud from a guidebook to Carolina Islands, he leaned down and felt the knot on his leg. At least that was not disappointing—a good solid lump.

He sat back in his seat, partially satisfied, and watched the road ahead.

"This is interesting," his mother was saying. "The loggerhead sea turtle comes ashore and lays eggs here. Wouldn't you love to see that?" She marked the page and turned. "Oh, and listen to this. Pirates used to hide in these islands and . . ."

"**I** am not going on any more rides," Deanie announced to her father.

Her father and Delores were sitting on a bench, eating Belgian waffles, laughing. Her father looked up at her, still smiling. "Why not?" There was whipped cream on his upper lip.

"Our boat got stuck in the Small World Tunnel, and we had to listen to a hundred and forty-five dolls singing 'It's a Small World After All' for—how long was it, Clara? I don't want to exaggerate."

"Two minutes," Clara said.

"It *must* have been longer than that. It seemed like hours. Anyway, dolls doing the same thing over and over are very boring." She broke off. "Oh, look, here come the Three Little Pigs."

"Where?" Clara asked. She moved back quickly

behind the bench and out of the reach of the Three Little Pigs. She had already been hugged by somebody in a Wimpy costume, and all she wanted now was to be left alone.

"Right there."

The Three Little Pigs came through the crowd singing "Who's Afraid of the Big Bad Wolf" and dancing on their short legs. They paused to circle an elderly couple. The old man gamely danced a jig with them.

Deanie turned back to her father. "Are those midgets in pig suits," she asked, "or little children?"

"They're real pigs," he answered.

Delores laughed, dropping Belgian waffle on her blouse. "Like me," she said, pointing to herself.

"See," Deanie's father went on, "the public won't accept real pigs dancing through the park, real pigs have a reputation for being slobs, so they put them in pink suits and false eyelashes. Do you think that old man would dance with that pig, if he knew she was real?"

"I think they're midgets," Deanie said, smiling, "like Munchkins."

"Well, anyway, Wimpy's a woman," Clara said loudly. "When she hugged me, I felt her chests!"

"Clara!" Deanie said. Clara paused, froze, and then turned away. Her father threw back his head and laughed. Delores choked on a piece of waffle and signaled to be clapped on the back.

Clara's face burned. Why had she said that? Chests! She looked around for a way to escape.

The Big Bad Wolf met her eyes. He was creeping through the crowd, making his way toward the Three Little Pigs. He put one finger to his lips. Don't tell! His eyebrows snapped up and down.

Clara twisted away. Suddenly she had to get away from it all—the confusion, the awful pretense of fun. How could the others keep it up? To Clara it was like a game in which they took turns making fun of one another.

A child's voice called out a warning to the pigs. "The Big Bad Wolf's behind that fat lady."

Clara walked quickly away from the bench. "Where are you going?" Deanie asked, following her.

"On a ride."

"Which one? We've been on everything. I hope you're not going to try to squeeze into the Tweety Bird Choo-Choo."

Clara looked up. Her eyes focused on the huge dome of the Space Cyclone, the one place nobody would follow her. "I'm going on that one," she said.

"Are you out of your mind? The Space Cyclone?"

"Yes."

"You know you'll get sick. Just once I would like to drive home from an amusement park with you when you didn't smell like puke. Dad, don't let her go!" Deanie turned back to her father, dodging people until she had his attention.

"Clara," her father called mildly, "don't go if it's going to make you sick."

Clara kept walking. "You're going to be miserable!" Deanie sang out behind her. Deanie's voice sounded so much like her mother's that Clara almost turned around to see if by some miracle her mother had actually arrived to take her home.

The Space Cyclone was just ahead. There was a sign warning people with bad hearts not to go on the ride. Clara handed the attendant her book, and he tore out the last ticket. Clara got into line.

There were three teen-age boys in front of her, a family of five behind. Clara was the only person who was not part of a group, but she was relieved to be alone. The line moved back and forth, snaking forward slowly. All too soon Clara was there. "Remove your sunglasses," a woman in a space outfit told her, "and remain seated until the end of the ride."

Clara nodded.

The car slid forward and slowly began to climb. It was so dark, Clara couldn't see anything. Space music

began. Computerized chords whined, rising and falling eerily. A cold came in the air.

Suddenly, without warning, the car lunged over the top and, twisting and turning, began to spiral down through the darkness. Clara heard herself scream. Stars exploded in her face. Meteorites flew at her. Space vehicles attacked. Her stomach turned as the car plunged down into a black hole and up again.

The car began another slow climb. Clara leaned back. She breathed deeply. She had never heard her body so loudly before. Blood pumped. Her ears popped. Her stomach throbbed. She was like an orchestra tuning up.

She screamed as the car went over the top again, screamed as it plunged—this time so steeply, Clara thought the car had actually come loose from its tracks and was hurtling through space.

She closed her eyes and clapped her hands over her ears. The music was mixed with human screams now, both building to a climax.

The car twisted, spiraled, dipped one last, sickening loop, and then straightened. It slid out into the light and stopped with a sure, mechanical click.

Clara bobbed forward in her seat. She opened her eyes. She felt as strange as an explorer seeing things for the first time. This is called light and these are people and you have just been on something called a ride.

The loudspeaker said, "Please step out of your car and walk through the door marked Reentry."

Clara tried to get to her feet, failed, and sat back in the space capsule. "Wasn't that awful?" a woman asked cheerfully as she passed.

"Yes," Clara answered. She got slowly to her feet and leaned over the car like a wilted flower.

"I'm going again as soon as I can get in line." The woman leaned closer. "Are you all right, honey? You look funny."

Clara smiled weakly. "I always look this way," she said. Stumbling slightly, she got out of the capsule and headed for Reentry.

John D was watching for Clara from a fake rock in front of the Volcano. His eyes were on the Space Cyclone exit.

John D felt that he alone knew the depth of Clara's misery. He alone understood what had made her go on the Space Cyclone.

He himself had spent the day moving from one event to another, watching mechanical apes square-dance, going under the sea in a pink submarine, riding through a huge sombrero where bulls sang,"Ay—yi—yi—yiiiii." Each good time had only made him more miserable.

When John D saw Clara come out, he straightened and stood up. She was the only person who didn't have someone to hold on to. His eyes narrowed.

All day long John D had felt as if he were in a pocket

of misery as individual as a crater on the moon, and now abruptly she was in it too. He watched her with the wary eyes of an animal whose burrow has just been invaded.

He usually considered people fools who made themselves more miserable than they had to be. Yet he felt a kinship with Clara. He himself had been hungry all day, but he had refused to eat anything.

Of course, that was different, he went on. He had not eaten because he wanted his mother to know he wasn't having a good time, and if she saw him wolfing down a hot fudge sundae, she would give him her See-I-Knew-You-Were-Having-Fun Look.

Anyway, his hunger pangs had been for nothing. His Mom had not glanced his way all day, not even when the attendant pinched his hand in the Pink Submarine hatch.

Suddenly he was ravenous. The sight of Clara leaning weakly against a Sylvester trash can made him feel strong and bursting with health.

"I'm going to the refreshment stand," he called cheerfully to his mother. She, Deanie, and Sam were walking toward him.

"John D," his mother called back, "we're going to stop at a nice restaurant on the way home. Please don't spoil your appetite."

He turned away with a careless wave and walked toward the refreshment stand.

How funny life was, he thought. Now he had made his mother miserable—and without even trying. A two-part misery, he thought with a small smile, since he definitely would spoil his appetite and "pick at his food," as she called it, in the nice restaurant.

This will make up, partially, he told himself, for her laughter when I fell into the car. He lifted his pant leg and looked at his bruise. He saw with disappointment that it was gone.

When I get back to the beach house, he decided, if I feel like it, I'll touch up the spot with lipstick and eyebrow pencil—that makes a perfect bruise—and then I'll put on shorts, come in the living room, and when she says, "What on earth happened to your leg?" I'll reply quietly, "This is the injury that gave you such amusement this morning."

The waitress said, "What'll you have?"

He looked up at the pictures. "A Mount Everest, I believe," he said. The picture showed a mountain of ice cream topped with chocolate sauce, cherries, pineapple, strawberries, nuts, and whipped cream. A small American flag was on top. His mother would flip. One of the reasons he loved junk food so much was because she hated it. She was always saying, "How can you eat that stuff? I can't even stand to watch."

He paid for his Mount Everest and carried it in both hands, like a waiter with a flaming dessert. He glanced up in time to see his mother's frown. That made him even hungrier.

"Oh, can I have a bite of that?" Deanie asked, coming forward with a sly smile.

He had not intended to share, but his Mount Everest was so big, there was no way he could hide it behind his back. He watched with obvious distaste as she scooped up whipped cream on one finger and licked it off. "Oh, that is sooooo good."

He tried to turn away, shielding his Mount Everest with his body. His spoon was in a plastic wrapper and he pulled at the plastic with his teeth.

"And may I have just one piece of pineapple?" She laughed as her fingers poked the pineapple deeper into the ice cream. "Oh, I'm making a mess."

"Indeed," he said coldly.

"Hold it steady."

The Mount Everest was halfway up his arm now, the flag disappearing into the whipped cream. He struggled with the plastic around the spoon.

"There. At last. Pineapple." Deanie turned, holding

the pineapple halfway to her lips. "Clara, you want a taste?"

Clara shook her head.

Mount Everest was melting. Chocolate syrup ran onto John D's arm. He looked around with the desperation of a dog with a bone.

"Come on, Clara. The whipped cream tastes just like melted marshmallows."

Clara, who was still leaning on the Sylvester trash can for support, shook her head quickly and looked away.

"You want to split something? I could go for a hot fudge sundae."

Again Clara shook her head. Then she looked up at the sky, down at her feet, around at the crowd. She inhaled, swallowed, looked around again, and then, as the others watched, turned, gagged, and vomited behind Sylvester's back.

"Well," John D said coldly to his mother, "you certainly don't have to worry about the *ice cream* spoiling my appetite."

"Are you all right, Clara?" his mother called.

John D stuck his spoon in the melted peak of Mount Everest and let the whole mountain slide into the nearest trash can. Then he wiped his hands on his shirt.

"Can we leave now?" he asked in the same cold voice.

"**A**re you sitting out here all by yourself for a reason?" Delores asked.

Clara's head jerked up. She had been sitting on the steps, watching the ocean and wishing she were at home. "No, no reason," she said quickly. "I'm just sitting here watching the waves." She had come out here to get away from everybody in the house but she knew not to say that.

"The ocean's so beautiful at night, isn't it?"

"Yes."

For a moment they both watched the beach. The foam-edged waves formed a white line along the shore. The even breaking of the waves made the kind of sound that lulls people to sleep.

Delores walked down three steps and sat beside Clara.

"You don't like to play Charades, do you?" Delores said.

"No."

"I gathered as much."

They had just finished a short game of Charades in which Clara had not guessed a single syllable. She had never cared much for pantomime, and the quickness required for Charades—the signals, the happy cries—"Title . . . TV show . . . three words . . . first syllable . . ." and the final triumphant "*Sha Na Na!*" Tonight it had seemed more like a bad dream than a game.

"I don't either usually," Delores went on. "It's too much like life, with everybody having trouble communicating. But—I don't know—here at the beach everything seems more fun, don't you think?" She hugged her knees and waited.

Clara could feel Delores looking at her. "I guess," she said. She turned her head away, casually, up the beach where the moon hung full and white over the sea.

"You aren't having a very good time, are you, Clara."

"It's all right."

"I know you didn't have fun at the amusement park yesterday."

"I like to swim," Clara said.

"Yes, you do seem to enjoy the ocean."

There was another awkward silence. Clara waited for Delores to go back into the house. Instead she heard Delores say, "I don't think John D's having a good time either."

Clara said "Oh" without interest.

"He doesn't make friends easily."

I bet, Clara thought. She kept looking at the moon. Anyway, who does make friends easily? Her eyes narrowed slightly, blurring the round moon.

What did adults expect? she wondered. They throw perfectly strange kids together and can't understand it when these perfectly strange kids don't become instant friends. Does anyone realize, she went on, that it has taken me my entire lifetime to find—in all the hundreds and hundreds of people in my school—two friends? Two!

"I wish you and John D could become friends," Delores went on. "I think you have a lot in common."

Clara turned and looked at Delores, her eyes wide open with surprise.

"I do think so. You're both serious and sensitive and have good minds. Your father's told me about your making Honor Society, and he's showed me some of your stories and poems."

Clara gasped. She turned away, no longer pretending

to be looking at the moon or the shore. She began breathing through her mouth. Her body had begun to need more air than her nose could inhale.

Delores said quickly, "I hope you don't mind your father sharing your stories with me. He's very proud of you."

Clara managed to say "No." She was as short of breath as if she had run a mile.

Clara had shared her writing with exactly four people in her life—her mother; her father; her best friend, Ellen, who wanted to be a writer; and her other friend, Jennifer, who was going to be an actress.

It was one of the few things Clara was particular about, private about. She did not let Deanie read her things—not that Deanie would want to—or even Mr. Fratiana, her English teacher, who kept telling her she ought to concentrate on her writing. She felt betrayed, deprived of something far more permanent than enough evening air.

The door opened behind them. "I'm trying to get someone to take a walk with me," her father said. "Deanie's washing her hair. John D's in his room. How about you two?"

"We'd love to. Come on, Clara." Delores got to her feet. "I love the beach at night." She laughed. "I'd love it in the daytime, too, if it weren't for all that sunshine."

Clara said, "I'm tired. I swam all afternoon and I think I'll go to bed."

"Just a short walk. Come on."

Clara got to her feet, and Delores's arm went around her shoulders companionably. They went down the steps like that, with Clara's father behind them. As they started over the dunes her father moved on the other side of Clara so that she was between them.

She clomped along the beach, feeling like a prisoner between guards. They talked over her head, laughed, and included her with an occasional, "Don't you think so, Clara?" And she answered with a noncommittal "I guess."

"I'm going back," she said suddenly, pulling away.

"Clara," her father pleaded. "Clarrie," his baby name for her.

"I'm tired," she said over her shoulder.

"Let's all go back," Delores said quickly. "Let's get blankets and lie out on the beach and pretend we know something about the stars."

Her father laughed. "I'm good at that. I spent my high-school dating years pointing out strange stars to girls. The only time my dates would sit close to me was for something scientific."

"I don't believe that, Sam. I've seen pictures of you in high school."

"It's true. I dreaded cloudy nights—whew, I'd just sit there with my palms getting sweaty."

"I cannot picture it. Pretend I'm— Oh, name me somebody you dated."

"Jo Ann Goodman."

"That name came awfully quickly. All right, pretend I'm Jo Ann Goodman and we're . . ."

Neither her father nor Delores noticed when Clara left them and went up to the house.

The gulls were screaming as Deanie and Clara came over the dunes, soaring evenly in the steady breeze that blew, this afternoon, from the north. Beyond them the pelicans crash-dived into the sea, scooped up fish, and flew away.

"Look how tan I'm getting," Deanie said. "Wait a minute till I take my rings off. There."

Out of the corner of her eye Clara could see her sister's shiny, buttered arms waving like a hula girl's. She kept her face turned toward the sea.

"I just hope I don't peel." She put her rings back on and stared with a pleased smile at her tan fingers.

Clara stomped through the marsh grass, stepped over a sign that forbade anyone to pick it, and moved onto the warm soft sand of the dunes. She was carrying an inflated air mattress under one arm.

Ahead the sea beckoned. The tide was going out. The waves lapped backward like a cat's tongue. There was a breeze, and the sea grass traced circles in the wind.

"Girls, don't go out too far," Delores called from the door of the beach house.

"We won't, Mommie," Deanie said to Clara in the tiny voice of a four-year-old.

"Girls, did you hear me?" Delores called louder, moving onto the steps.

The girls paused at the edge of the dunes. Behind them the cabbage palms and scrub pines cast a short shadow. It was three o'clock.

Deanie smiled and waved. "We heard," she called. "We won't."

As they started walking Deanie's smile faded. "I'm getting so tired of her. How many pairs of designer jeans does she have?"

"Many."

"And did you watch her last night when we were playing Charades?"

Clara shook her head. The float trailed in the soft sand behind her.

"Well, the whole time I was acting out *Close*

Encounters of the Third Kind, Dear Delores was having close encounters of her own. She was leaning over Dad and breathing on him. She acts like Wanda Jeanine Raye in my high school."

"I am so stupid," Clara said suddenly.

Deanie looked at her in surprise. "What brought that on?"

"Nothing."

"You're not stupid. You make good grades."

"Grades," Clara said in the same flat voice.

"Listen, I finally figured it out. This may make you feel better. Everyone in the world is stupid. The Queen of England is stupid. Walter Cronkite is stupid. The Pope is stupid. The only difference is that they are all stupid less of the time than other people. I'm not good at percents but, say, Walter Cronkite is probably stupid five percent of the time. We are probably stupid fifteen percent of the time."

"A hundred percent is more like it for me."

"I wish you wouldn't do that."

"What?"

"Depress me. It makes me frown, and then I don't tan in my wrinkles."

"I—"

"Anyway, I've seen stars, *stars* come on talk shows

and be more stupid than we'd ever be. I saw Bonnie Franklin talk to Dinah Shore about cold sores, and cold sores have to be the most stupid thing there is."

"I'm going swimming," Clara said abruptly. She began to run toward the water. She hopped on one foot as she stepped on a sharp shell and then ran again.

"Remember, don't go out too far!" Deanie called. One of her main pleasures these days was imitating Delores. She had it down perfectly. "Clara, did you hear your new mommie?"

She broke off when there was no acknowledgment of her imitation. She stood watching Clara run through the shallow waves.

Then, with a sigh, she began turning around slowly, as if she were on a spit, so that all sides of her body would get an even tan. With her arms out to her sides, she was like a figure on a music box.

Clara jumped over the first wave, lifted the float higher, waded between waves, turned sideways as the next wave broke over her. She felt pleasure in struggling with the waves, her first pleasure of the day. It was as if she were getting over a barrier, away from something, and on to something new at the same time.

The water deepened. Clara felt herself step down a sandy slope. Every day the ocean changed. Every day was different. Sand swirled around her ankles.

A wave struck the side of her head. She tasted salt, and shook her head to get the water out of her ear. Then the wave rippled past, pulling at the float, rolling over itself onto the shore.

Clara felt for a secure bottom with her feet. The current was tugging at her ankles. Then a gentle wave came, lifted her, put her back down.

Another wave was coming. Clara faced it. Lots of foam and power in this one, she thought. With renewed energy, Clara got set to rise above it.

John D was sitting on the porch in a rocking chair, writing intently in his brown spiral notebook. He glanced up to make sure the girls were really at the beach and not sneaking back to the house to catch him at his work.

He relaxed. He had the house to himself now. His mom and Sam had left for the fish market.

"I'm going to make my famous Shrimp Mornay," his mother had announced as they were leaving.

He had stared at her. He had never heard of such a dish. He wondered if she had some recipes hidden in her suitcase. He had spent a few pleasant moments imagining his mom with the recipe hidden in her palm, like somebody cheating on a test, casually tossing together her creation.

Maybe his mom did know how to make Shrimp whatever. After all she was perfect at everything else—

the perfect newspaper columnist, the perfect mother. He smiled. The proof of that was that he had turned out to be a perfect child.

He was on Chapter Six of his book now. He was going to dedicate it to the girls.

"To Deanie and Clara," it would read, "without whose idiotic behavior I could never have written this chapter." He was proud of that and circled the period at the end.

The title was "How to Conceal the Fact That You Are an Idiot: Ten Simple, Basic Rules of Behavior That Will Conceal the Stupidity That Lurks in All of You." He did not write "in All of *Us*" because he felt no stupidity lurked in him.

He straightened, squaring his shoulders beneath his T-shirt. He was, he felt, back to his usual intelligent, superior self. A momentary setback—that was how he now thought of the events of the past days—the undeserved humiliation, the unfair scorn. Even Einstein must have had such days. After all, there were idiotic girls back then too.

It was like having a disease, he decided, a disease that weakened you but then—this was the good part— made you immune, so that you never had to worry about getting that disease again.

He looked up. Clara was in the water, struggling

through the waves with her yellow float. Now she was holding it behind her like a cape. She turned sideways as the next wave hit, and the float turned over, showing its red underside.

On the beach Deanie was doing something strange. She was standing in place, turning slowly with her arms out to the sides, her face lifted to the sun. It was like a slow, weary tribal dance.

John D went back to watching Clara. She was beyond the breakers now, trying to get onto the float. She struggled, rose, and flopped onto the float sideways. She paused while the float rose on a swell. Then she threw one leg over the yellow plastic, then the other. She stretched out.

With her hands on either side, she began to paddle idly, keeping herself just beyond the breakers, inside the swells.

Since obviously the girls were going to be entertaining themselves in this juvenile fashion for hours—turning in place and lying on a float—John D went back to his writing.

He was writing rule four for concealing stupidity. "Refrain from laughing at people."

He looked at what he had written for a moment. Then he added, "It is entirely possible that you will be laughing at someone more intelligent than yourself, someone far superior." He hesitated, then added for emphasis, "I myself have been ridiculed. All great men have been. But truly intelligent people never laugh at others. It is a certain sign of stupidity."

He glanced up, over the shells the girls had found on the beach and lined along the porch railing—the conchs, the angel's wings, the periwinkles, the olives, the green sand dollar.

He remembered the pleasure of watching Clara's smile fade as she had come running in calling, "Look! I found a *green* sand dollar!"

"The reason it's green," he'd said quietly, "is because it's still alive—or *was*." A perfect put-down.

He noticed that Deanie had now added arm movements to her endless, boring turning. She was flexing her arms in and out, possibly one of those cheerleading gestures she was so fond of, John D thought. While her arms pumped in and out, her feet continued their slow turning. She was like a mechanical doll gone wild—legs moving slower and slower, arms about to fly off her body.

When he finished this chapter, he decided, he was going to write one called "How to Stop Being Boring." Only he, who had never, ever, not once bored himself in his whole life, could write such a chapter without—he smiled—being boring.

Clara lay with her head resting on her arms. Her eyes were closed. The smooth, rhythmic rise and fall of the waves soothed her. She felt at peace for the first time since she had arrived at the beach. The world liked her after all, she thought. It had taken her, a troubled child, onto its lap and was rocking her, soothing her.

She was glad she had found the float that morning in the hall closet, all bunched up in a plastic ball; glad she had spent the morning straightening it out, blowing it up. She smiled slightly. Puffy cheeks are good for something after all, she told herself.

The sun was warm on her back. The water that lapped over the sides of the float was cool on her stomach. She dipped her hands into the water and made a few strokes to keep the float from drifting back into the breakers. Then she folded her arms back under her cheek.

Overhead the gulls were crying. The sound seemed soothing now. She was sleepy, relaxed.

She lifted her head. The float was in the same spot, had not drifted either way. She dipped her arms into the water, paddling slowly, idly. She watched the shore, the long white curving beach, the dunes blown up from the beach into a double line. The dunes had overtaken the trees in some places, and the twisted trunks stuck up in the sand.

Clara closed her eyes. I think I'll just stay out here until it's time to go home, she thought. A week on a raft. She would write a book about it like John D— *How I Avoided Embarrassment and Personal Misery and Attained Peace and a Union with Nature in Seven Days on a Raft: A Story of Inspiration and Courage* by Clara Malcolm.

She wondered idly what John D's book was about. She knew he was writing one because she had seen *Chapter Two* at the top of a page, and then the words *How to—*. Probably "How to Bring Misery and Discomfort to Those Around You," she decided. "Twenty Ways to Make People Feel Awful, with a Special Pictorial Section on Insulting Looks."

And, she went on, her father's book would be *How*

to Have a Vacation with Your Daughters Without Noticing They Are Present. She frowned slightly, opened her eyes, and stared at the waves.

And Delores. Clara paused, waiting to think of what her book would be. *How to Ruin the Vacation of the Daughters of the Man You Love.* It would be the shortest book in the world—one sentence. "Go along on their vacation."

Clara blinked her eyes against the glare. The salt spray had dried on her arms, giving a frosted look to her skin. She touched her arm with her tongue, tasted salt. She closed her eyes.

She would put all the books together in a box, like a set, she decided, and the set would be called *Two Weeks in*—she paused—*Two Weeks in the Wrong Place with the Wrong People.* She sighed. *At the Wrong Time for the Wrong Reasons.*

She lay without moving, her hands trailing in the water. She could hear the waves breaking on the shore, but it was like the distant boom of thunder. Her breathing grew regular. She drifted toward sleep. "Mnnn," she sighed.

On the shore Deanie continued to turn in place. Her eyes were closed, her face lifted to the sun. Her feet were wearing a circular pattern in the sand.

On the porch John D continued writing his rules for

concealing stupidity. He paused, pushed his glasses up on his nose, and waited for inspiration. Then, abruptly, he began writing again.

Clara's float, borne now as easily, as lightly, as a toy, moved, rose, fell, shifted, turned, and bobbed idly on the waves.

John D had completed rule five for concealing stupidity. It was "Avoid the physical appearance of a fool. Don't let your mouth hang open. Don't put your fingers in your nose. Don't scratch your head when you're thinking. Don't spill food on yourself and others. Don't wipe your nose on your shirt. Don't say 'Duh' when you don't know the answer."

He left space after his last *Don't* because he knew he would think of a lot more.

He looked up from his paper as satisfied as if he had eaten a five-course meal. He saw that Deanie had abandoned her arm movements and was standing quietly, facing south.

As John D watched she took three steps and stopped when she faced west. She would have been looking right at the house and John D if her eyes had been open.

"Boring," John D said.

He looked at the ocean, but he did not see Clara. He got to his feet. He glanced up and down the beach. She was not in sight. He moved to the edge of the porch so that he had a better view. No Clara.

He felt foolish, like one of those parents who rush out to search frantically for the missing child who turns out to be watching TV at Billy's house. He walked to the steps, opened the screen door, stepped outside. No Clara. He felt a sudden pang of anxiety.

He walked quickly down the steps, past the clothes-line of bathing suits. A lizard scurried across his path. A bird flew out of the sea grass. John D did not notice them. He stretched and strained like a tourist for a glimpse of the yellow float.

Holding his pencil idly, like a forgotten cigar, he moved to the dunes. The wind blew his hair across his face. He brushed it aside. The pencil dropped unnoticed from his hand.

Now, atop the dunes, he could see a mile in either direction. The beach was empty, a long flat stretch of white. Not even a fisherman in sight. Only Deanie, slowly turning in the afternoon sun, broke the view.

John D raised one hand to shade his eyes and looked

out to sea. He thought he saw a spot of yellow on the horizon. His eyes narrowed behind his heavy glasses. He lifted his glasses. He could see better from a distance without them.

He stepped forward. No, it was gone—or else it had never been there.

He resettled his glasses and ran down the dunes, slipping in the soft hot sand. He went down on one knee. He scrambled up, crossed the beach, and stopped in front of Deanie, who was now facing north. There was a faint smile on her face, as if she were listening to a favorite song.

"Where's your sister?" he asked abruptly.

"Oh, don't do that!" Deanie's eyes snapped open. She put her hands over her bathing suit top. "You scared me to death! You should never, ever, come up on somebody who's"—she hesitated, looking for the right word— "who's thinking about something and yell at them."

"Where is Clara?"

He was so close to her that he could smell the sickening odor of hot tanning butter and sweat. He wanted to shake some sense into her, but she was too disgusting to touch.

"Clara? She's—"

Deanie turned to face the ocean and then she looked blankly up and down the beach. Her greased fingers were still clasped over her heart. Her eyes began to blink.

"She was right here a minute ago—on the raft."

"I know that. I saw that. Where is she now?"

"Are you sure she didn't come up to the house?"

"Yes, I am sure she didn't come up to the house."

"Well, you don't have to sound like that."

"I'll sound anyway I want to."

"You think you are *so* perfect," Deanie sneered. "You think you can come down here like Mr. Superiority and tell us—"

"Don't you realize," he interrupted in a voice so cold that Deanie broke off her words and looked at him, "that while you have been out here turning around and around like a hunk of barbecue meat, your sister has been swept out to sea?"

Deanie stepped backward out of the hole she had worn in the sand, leaving it between them. Her sudden silence, her blinking eyes, her gaping mouth, brought John D no satisfaction at all.

Clara awoke with a start as a spray of cold water slapped across her back. She lifted her head and looked around in irritation.

She saw the swell of a wave rising behind her, the white crest of foam. For a moment Clara thought she had drifted into the breakers and was about to be washed up onto the beach. She looked ahead to see how close the beach was. She saw another wave.

A cold fear gripped her. These were not the long gentle waves of the shore, but the dark choppy waters of the sea. Her shoulders tightened. She gasped air into her lungs. Slowly, holding on to the float with tight cold hands, she lifted her head.

There were only waves, rising then falling to reveal more waves. She turned and glanced over her shoulder. A wave broke over her legs and sent cold spray across her back again. She ducked her head. She waited tensely, afraid to move.

As the float rose on the crest of the next wave, she lifted her head and saw the faint gray line of the shore on the horizon. The solid hump of the hotels, stores, and houses at the end of the island told her how far away she had drifted.

She began to paddle. Her arms dipped into the sea again and again, her cupped hands pulling through the cold water. She did not look up, just kept drawing her arms mechanically through the sea like a swimmer. Spray slapped across her face, but she did not stop to wipe it away. When she paused, finally, to rest her trembling arms, she looked up and saw the shore was no nearer.

She put her head down. She lay with her eyes closed, blocking the sea, the waves, the distant island, from her mind.

Suddenly the sun went behind a cloud, and Clara felt the chill of the wind. Her teeth began to chatter, her legs to shake. The float wiggled unsteadily, too, and Clara clutched the sides. She tried to breathe deeply, regularly. Stay calm, she told herself. A spray of water hit her face, and she spit out saltwater. Stay calm, she repeated.

There was nothing gentle or comforting about the

sea now. This was no mother comforting a child. This was a mean hang-on-if-you-can kind of motion.

Suddenly Clara heard the sound of an engine. Her spirits surged. Her head snapped up. A boat was on the horizon.

"Over here!" she screamed, waving her arm. "Help me. I'm over here!"

It was a cabin cruiser, moving steadily toward the island, rolling slightly with the motion of the waves. Clara could see a man on deck, facing away from her, into the wind.

"Help! I'm over here! *Help!*"

How could he not hear her? Clara struggled to sit up on the float. "I'm over here. I'm—" Suddenly the float flexed over a wave and bucked like a horse. Clara yelped, flopped down, and clutched the plastic. When the motion of the float was steady again, she raised her head.

"I'm over here!"

The boat had already moved past her. She could smell the fumes from the exhaust. The sound of the engine was growing fainter. The man on deck had gone into the cabin.

"Come back!" she yelled louder. "Help me! Come back!"

The boat grew smaller, the sound fainter, and Clara's shoulders sagged. Her nose began to run.

Then she lowered her head and started crying, making no effort to wipe her wet face. "Why didn't he see me?" she moaned.

Suddenly a wave hit the float broadside. The float rose, dipped with a sickening lunge, and rose again. Clara felt her stomach twist with nausea. She tightened her hold. As the float rose again, she closed her eyes and waited for the sickness to pass.

A second wave broke over the side of the float, and water filled her nostrils. She choked and gagged. And as she threw back her head for air she saw there was nothing in sight now but the sea. She was overcome with a kind of loneliness she had only read about.

She twisted in a desperate move, churning the water with her hands, turning the float around. There was the island. The lighthouse. She felt a moment of relief.

She thought she heard another boat. She raised her head. There had to be boats! There were hundreds in the marina. She waited, but the only sound she heard now was the waves.

There was an unreal feeling to it all, she thought, as she searched the horizon for boats. Her eyes stung with salt and tears. It was as if she had gone to sleep in one ocean and awakened in another.

She began to paddle again, moving her arms through

the cold water. This made her feel better, more in control. She kept her head down so she could not see that she was not getting closer to the island. Indeed, the island seemed to be drifting farther away.

"I still do not believe Clara has been carried out to sea," Deanie said stubbornly.

"Then you are completely free to return to the beach house and resume your ridiculous sunbathing routine," John D said.

He did not bother to look at her. He felt he had already seen the two expressions she was capable of— pleasure in herself and irritation with others—and both annoyed him.

Deanie and John D were walking down the middle of the deserted road that led to town and the only telephones on the island. No car had passed since they started walking.

"You should have kept an eye on her," John D said, watching the road ahead that still wavered with the day's heat. On either side of the road grew beach peas and stunted goldenrod.

"Me?"

"Yes, you."

"You don't have any right to speak to me like that."

"I'll speak to you any way I choose."

She glanced at him, wanting to lecture him again on trying to act superior. Something about the set of his chin decided her against it.

"Anyway," she went on, "there was no reason to 'keep an eye on her,' as you put it. My sister is not a baby."

"Your sister was in a very miserable state of mind," he said.

"Clara?"

"Yes, Clarrra." He clamped his lips shut as he heard his own tone of voice.

"Clara was not miserable."

"She was too."

"She's my sister, and I say she was not miserable!"

They glared at each other over the sand-blown pavement. John D said, "One, she does not eat. Two, she does not talk. Three, she wants to be by herself all the time. Four, she went on the Space Cyclone knowing it would make her sick because she had to get away from everybody."

Deanie's eyes blinked rapidly four times. "Well," she said, "Mr. Expert on Human Behavior, if she *was* miserable, it was because you and your stupid mother wormed your way into our vacation."

"I myself was dragged here."

John D pushed his glasses up on his nose angrily. He stood and watched her walk away. The only sound was the slap of her thongs against the sandy pavement.

Suddenly there was the sound of an approaching car. John D spun around. An old rusty Dodge was coming. John D held out his arms to keep it from passing.

When the car lurched to a stop, John D said, "Could we get a ride into town? We think her sister's been carried out to sea on a float. We need help." He was proud his voice was calm.

"Well, get in," the man said. As John D and Deanie crawled into the backseat over the fishing equipment, he added, "It's been a bad year for drownings."

In a bucket at John D's feet blue crabs scratched against the metal. The smell of old fish and seawater choked him. He swallowed.

"A drowning," he said carefully, "is what we are trying to prevent."

"There was a man drowned in June," the man went on, throwing the car in gear, "and a lady back in May."

"Someone should keep an eye on these people," said John D. He was watching the back of the man's neck, but out of the corner of his eye he noticed a quick movement as Deanie glanced at him. Expression Number Two, he thought, irritation with others.

"It don't matter whether you keep an eye on them or not," the man said. "The woman's husband was sitting on the beach, and he couldn't do a thing. They found the man's body, but they never did find hers."

John D did not answer. He felt as if he had been drawn into a strong unknown current himself, swept out of a safe harbor into dangerous waters, and he was helpless to change his direction.

He did not want to care about Clara, or about anybody else for that matter. He wanted only to act calmly, sanely, deliberately, the way he would act to save the life of any stranger. He felt he *was* acting that way, but underneath, where it counted, he was neither cool nor calm.

"Where was your folks when this happened?" the man asked.

"They went to get shrimp," Deanie said.

"What kind of car was they driving?"

"Mercedes," John D answered.

John D looked out the window. The sun was getting

113

lower in the sky now, low enough to shine in the car window. He shielded his eyes. Dark clouds were moving in from the north. The moss on the live oaks was blowing in the wind.

As he sat there, eyes shaded, jaw tense, he felt a chill go through him. He actually shuddered, something he had never done before in his life.

"What's wrong with you?" Deanie snapped.

"Nothing!"

He hated the thought of night coming on, of bad weather approaching. He hated the helplessness of human beings, of Clara being battered about like an insignificant twig, of himself being battered around inside.

He had always had a respect for the ocean. Other people might think of it as something for ships to sail on or something to swim at the edge of or something to dump wastes in. He saw it as a colossal, mysterious force that man would never understand.

They were coming into town now. They passed the bait shop, the shell shop where conch-shell lamps glowed in the window, passed the café where you could eat all the fish you wanted for $2.95, past the trailer park. They drove slowly, searching the parking lots.

"There they are! There they are!" John D cried as he

saw an approaching cream Mercedes. "Stop!" He fumbled with the door handle. "Stop the car!"

"I am!" The man stomped on the brake four times. "There, I'm stopped."

The door handle was twisting uselessly in John D's hand.

"That door don't work. You'll have to get out on her side."

John D tried to climb over Deanie, but she shoved him back with surprising strength. "She's *my* sister," she said.

She got out of the car and ran down the middle of the road, waving frantically. "Daddy! Daddy!"

"She's going to get killed herself," the man said. "Now, wouldn't that be something? One drowned and one run over?"

John D did not answer. He waited with one hand over his pounding heart. The car stopped.

Deanie paused in the center of the road while her father and Delores got out of the car and ran toward her.

"They're all going to get hit," the man predicted cheerfully.

"Clara's been swept out to sea!" Deanie cried. Then she burst into tears. As her father bent toward her, his face gone ashen in a moment, John D crawled out of the backseat.

The traffic had stopped now. Drivers and passengers watched them with curiosity.

"Thanks for the ride," John D said. With his hand still firmly on his chest, holding his emotions in place, he walked through the cars to join them.

Clara had been clinging to the float for two hours. She no longer yelled or cried or paddled toward the retreating island. She lay with her eyes squeezed shut, her body as stiff and unmoving as one of those bodies uncovered in Pompeii, petrified in a moment of fear.

The waves were high and choppy now, and there was no rhythm to the movements of the float. It was like an amusement park ride designed to keep people off-balance. The float went up, turned sideways, tipped, was hit broadside by waves, slid between waves—up, down, sideways.

Occasionally when the float made a particularly wrenching move, Clara would moan, but it was the sound of someone beyond hope. She had long since given up any thought of rescue. She felt as if she had been drawn far away from the normal world, into one of those spots that sailors fear, where the sea ignores the laws of nature and goes wild, a spot marked on old maps by drawings of dragons and reptiles.

Clara had no idea how long she had been on the raft —all her life, it seemed. The part of her life spent on dry land—walking, sleeping, eating, doing normal things—seemed like a brief vague dream. This was hard cold reality.

A wave slapped against the float, and Clara suddenly felt it tipping over. She screamed and clutched the raft tighter, but her scream was cut short. The raft flipped over and Clara was thrown into the sea.

Her head went under water, and she came up choking. She slung her wet hair from her face and looked around. The float was drifting away.

Clara swam after it. She reached out. The current pulled the float just beyond her grasp. She struggled through the waves, her eyes on the float, gasping for breath, swallowing saltwater.

Her fingers touched the corner of the float and she fumbled to hold it. The float slipped away on the crest of a wave. She touched it again. It was gone. It was as if a playful hand were jerking the float out of her reach.

Clara began to swim. Another wave rose and she sank into the trough between waves. The float was out of sight. Clara was gripped with a terrible fear.

She waited, treading water anxiously, her eyes on the rolling waves. She caught sight of the float then, on the crest of a wave, and she struck out. Her arms and legs moved with a strength she had not known she had. Her teeth were clenched, her mouth clamped shut. A wave hit her face, and she plunged through it. She was gaining.

She swam again, lifting her head. The float was within reach. She scissored her legs in one last spurt and felt her fingers close on the thin plastic. Tears ran down her cheeks as she pulled herself up.

She lay across the float for a moment, her legs trailing in the choppy water. She coughed. She was exhausted. Her strength had gone as quickly as it had come. She could not lift her legs onto the float.

As she lay there, arms and legs trembling with fatigue and cold, she noticed something printed on the float. She blinked her eyes to clear them. NOT TO BE USED AS A LIFE PRESERVER, she read. She rested her face against the letters. Now they tell me. She closed her stinging eyes.

Then slowly, gasping with the effort, she threw one leg over the float. She rested. She pulled the other leg up and stretched out as gingerly as an old dog. She closed her eyes. Her heart was pounding in her ears.

She lay there, clutching the sides of the float with

both hands, legs shaking, knees knocking, waiting tensely for the next wave that could throw her again into the sea.

This time, she said through her clenched teeth, this time I won't let go.

She glanced over her shoulder. The waves were tinted red by the sinking sun. She glanced skyward. The clouds were moving in, gray and foreboding. A lone gull, white as snow, dipped in the darkening sky.

I will not let go, she said again.

John D and his mother sat on the plastic sofa in the office of the Coast Guard. The cushions were stiff and uneven, and they sat on the edge of their seats like unwanted guests. A cup of cold coffee was in his mother's hand, forgotten.

At the desk, waiting by the radio, were Deanie and her father. He was leaning forward, hand over his eyes as if shielding them from too much light. His shoulders were hunched up stiffly under his thin shirt. Deanie was twisting her hair.

"What did that man say?" Deanie asked as a garbled message came from the radio. Both she and her father leaned forward.

"It wasn't about your daughter, sir," the man answered in a kind voice.

"Why can't they find her?"

"Every ship we have is on the alert, every fishing boat's been contacted, two helicopters are searching the area."

"I know, but she can't have gotten that far. It's only been three hours."

"They know where to look, sir. They know the tides." He paused. "I'll let you know as soon as we hear something." He waited as if he expected them to move away, but they remained hunched miserably over the desk.

Across the room Delores sighed. "I absolutely cannot bear to think of Clara out there on a flimsy raft. She must be terrified."

"I should think," John D answered tersely.

"You know"—her voice lowered—"I have always had a real dread of the ocean. I admit it. I have the feeling when I'm swimming that there are, I don't know, *creatures* under there."

"There are, Mother."

"And the thought of being out there on a raft!" Her voice lowered again. "John D, that kind of raft costs five dollars. It is made of the cheapest, flimsiest plastic there is!"

"I know!" John D always spoke with special anger when his mother said exactly what he himself was thinking.

"I should never have let her go out."

"Mom, it was not your fault." He got up abruptly and walked to the desk. He stood behind Deanie, waiting to be noticed. "Any news?" he asked finally.

Deanie glanced around. In her anxiety she had twisted her hair into long uneven curls, and her face looked like something out of an old album. "No," she said. John D waited a moment more, then turned and walked to the window. He looked out.

Beyond the bay and the tidal marsh and the live oaks and the palmettos, the sun was beginning to sink in the sky. John D watched as it moved closer to the treetops and turned the water red.

The boats rose and fell in the marina. White yachts, sailboats, double-deck cruisers, old fishing boats, all wallowed on the waves. The water was getting rougher, John D noticed.

He crossed the room, got a drink of water he didn't want, and sat by his mother. He flopped down so hard that his mother bounced.

"No news?" she asked.

"No."

His mother took a sip of her cold coffee. "It has always bothered me terribly to think of somebody who is trapped. I can hardly read stories about people who are stuck in mines or submarines. And now Clara—I can't bear it."

She broke off as another message came over the radio. The operator looked up and shook his head. It was not about Clara. "There was a dreadful story last summer," she went on. "A man, in the Pacific, I believe, fell overboard, and ship after ship went right past him. A liner almost bumped into him."

"That won't happen with Clara," he said. He sometimes felt that in hard times he and his mother switched places. He became the calming adult, saying, "That won't happen" and "Everything will be all right," while she thought up new worries.

"I should never have let her go out on that raft."

"Mom."

"I shouldn't have. I did a whole column on it once— on not letting your child's life depend on a two-dollar piece of inflated plastic. I had had this heartbreaking letter from a woman whose child—they were in a lake —and she turned her back just for a moment and—"

"Mom."

"You know why I didn't?" She paused. "Because I wanted the girls to like me, and I was afraid if I kept saying over and over, 'Be careful, Don't do this, Stop that,' well—only look! They don't like me at all."

"They like you."

"They don't. So I might as well have played the part

of the Wicked Stepmother. At least Clara would be safe."

The radio was transmitting again, and the operator leaned close. Deanie and her father strained to hear. John D got up quickly and crossed the room.

"Go ahead. . . . Yes . . ."

Clara's father drew his shoulders up under his thin shirt as if he were preparing to take a blow. Deanie reached for his arm.

"I see. . . . How far out? . . . What color was it? . . . Any sign of the girl? . . . I see."

There was a long pause, then the man said, "Discontinue search."

"What?" Deanie asked in the sudden stillness. "Discontinue?"

The man remained at the silent radio, bent forward, eyes on the dials. Then he looked up at Clara's father. He took off his cap. He made a gesture with his head, a sideways nod, as if he were trying to rid himself of a troubling thought.

"The helicopter spotted the raft," he said. "Your daughter wasn't on it."

Deanie was in the bathroom of the Coast Guard station, standing in the middle of the tiled floor. She was alone. Delores had tried to come in with her, but Deanie had fought with Delores, struggled, and hit her, crying "Let me alone!" so violently that Delores had at last stepped back, arms raised in a gesture of defeat, and let her go into the bathroom alone.

Now that she had won the battle and was alone, Deanie felt even more miserable. She looked around at the drab walls, the toilets, the basins. She had never understood why anyone would ever actually choose to be alone. She squeezed her eyes shut, turned her face to the ceiling, opened her eyes, and looked in misery at the lone light fixture.

She heard the door open behind her. "It's me," Delores said from the doorway. "May I come in?"

"No," Deanie said.

She heard Delores's footsteps on the tile floor, coming toward her. She was relieved, but she let out her breath in a long sigh of pain and frustration.

"Where is my father?" she asked.

"He's trying to get your mom on the phone."

Suddenly Deanie sagged. Her shoulders slumped. If there had been anything to hold on to for support, she would have grabbed it. "I feel awful," she said.

"I know you do, but you have to realize—"

Deanie turned and faced Delores. "Did you ever have a sister?"

"A half sister, but she was ten years older than I, and we weren't close."

"Then you wouldn't understand," Deanie said flatly. She turned away, walked to one of the basins, and leaned.

She could see her face in the warped mirror over the basin. Her face was as hard as a mask, her hair twisted like snakes.

"I probably wouldn't have understood it yesterday myself," she admitted.

She turned around. Still leaning on the basin, she said, "I mean, you just don't believe your sister is going to get pulled out to sea. I mean, sure, bad things happen. Sure, people drown. But not your own sister!"

"I know."

"I mean, if you believed something like that would happen, well, you would never be mean or leave her out or—" She broke off. "I mean, I never ever thought anything would happen to Clara!"

She clamped her lips shut. Suddenly she wished she could cry. She felt the tears building inside her. She put her fists to her eyes and pressed.

Delores said, "My husband—John D's father—was killed in a plane crash the day he was born. He was flying to the hospital to be with me, and the plane crashed in Pittsburgh. He died a half hour before John D was born."

Deanie dropped her hands and looked at Delores. Delores had spoken so softly that Deanie moved closer. "That really happened?"

"I was just like you. I couldn't believe it. Things like that didn't happen."

"I know."

"Well, when I did believe it, I went to pieces. I wouldn't even hold John D for weeks. The nurses kept bringing him in and bringing him in and—to me it was as if, well, if John D hadn't been born early, then John would never have been on that plane and would never have crashed. He would still be alive." She shook her head. "It sounds awful, I know, inhuman, but at the time . . ."

"Does John D know about that?"

"He knows his father died on the day he was born, and he knows I went sort of crazy." She sighed. "John D's a very bright boy. He doesn't miss much."

"I'm sorry for the way I've been acting."

"It's all right." She put her hands on Deanie's shoulders. "I do know how you feel." When Deanie did not pull away, she slid her arms around her.

"I said something that was so true the other day," Deanie said.

"What was that?"

"I said that what's really wrong with the world is that things happen to the wrong people. I mean"—her voice began to quiver—"I mean, like the wrong people get sick and die and swept out to sea."

"I've felt like that."

"Clara's really a better person than I am, if you want to know the truth."

And Deanie put her head on Delores's shoulder and began to cry.

will not let go. . . . I will not let go. . . .

Clara was so intent on staying on the raft that she had not heard the sound of the approaching boat. She had not heard the men's voices.

"Hey, girl, are you all right?"

"She's not moving."

"She's got to be alive. Look how tightly she's holding on."

I will not let go. . . .

Clara had not seen the boat pull up behind her, did not feel the raft bump against the boat. And when human hands grabbed her stiff arm, she screamed like a wild person. "Nooooo!" She flung her head back, still screaming, and was lifted out of the water like something baited and caught from the sea.

She was clutching the float so tightly that it came out of the water with her. When the men lifted her over the side, it flopped back into the water and bobbed away on the choppy sea.

Clara grabbed at the air, but the man said, "You don't need that anymore. You're all right. You're with us."

She was on her knees, staring around, blank-eyed.

"You're all right," he said in a softer voice. "Get a blanket," he told someone.

Clara began to shiver. Her teeth clattered. She wrapped her arms around herself.

"Here, here."

Still on her knees, still shaking violently, Clara was wrapped in a blanket and helped to her feet. When her trembling legs would not support her, she was lifted and carried below and put on a bunk.

There she realized for the first time that she had been saved. She began to cry, sobbing into the blanket, shivering harder than ever.

"It's all right," the man said. He was rubbing her arms now, trying to get some heat into her body. "You're on our boat. We're taking you to the island."

He spoke in the soothing tone people use to calm frightened animals. "We aren't a half hour from the bay. You'll be home soon."

Clara nodded, then lifted her head. "Thank you," she said through her salt-parched lips.

"I bet your parents are worried sick. We'd call ahead, but our radio's out."

"It's just my father and sister."

"Well, I know they're worried sick. How did it happen?"

"I don't know. One minute I was floating by the beach and I closed my eyes and when I woke up—well, I was out where you found me."

Suddenly Clara sat up. "I want to go up on deck," she said.

"Well, now, I don't know whether you ought to be doing that or not," the man said. "You just—"

"I want to see the ocean. I have to."

"Well, wrap up." The man tightened the blanket around her, threw a towel over her head, and helped her up the narrow steps.

As they came onto the deck the man said, "There's a helicopter. It was probably searching for you."

"If they know I'm gone."

"They know."

Clara sat in one of the chairs and pulled her legs up under the blanket. There was the island—the lighthouse, the long curving shore. Then she let her eyes look back at the sea.

"Sea's getting higher," the man said.

Clara nodded, her eyes on the waves.

From the boat the waves looked high and rolling, with an occasional crest of foam, but not a dangerous sea. Then the boat dipped between waves, wavered, and Clara clutched the arms of her chair. As the boat lunged forward she shuddered.

"Cold?"

"No." She licked her upper lip and tasted salt. She looked at the man. "I'm just—" She paused to find the right word, realized there wasn't one, and substituted "glad." She smiled.

"This has been quite a day for us, young lady. I was thinking, before we spotted you, that I had something to brag about—we caught more than a hundred blues today. Now I really got something to brag about. It's been quite a day."

"For me too," Clara said.

The boat moved over the waves, and Clara leaned forward in her seat. She watched the water with a new kind of intensity. They rounded the end of the island, and Clara rose from her seat as they came into the bay.

John D was standing at the window alone, watching the boats coming into the bay, their masts sharp against the darkening sky. He had no right to feel sad, he told himself. Deanie had made that clear in the car with her fierce "She's *my* sister!" It was as if you weren't allowed to feel grief unless you met certain family conditions.

Actually, he thought, I probably don't qualify. I only knew Clara one week. She was scared of me. I looked down on her. The Animal. Only I still feel bad, terrible actually.

He could see in the window the reflection of the room behind him. Clara's father was at the desk, still trying to put through a call to Clara's mother.

In the past half hour Sam had changed from a neat, controlled man into the picture of despair. His thin hair stood up like wire; his clothes had come untucked; his eyes were red and swollen.

Delores sat on the sofa with one arm around Deanie, patting her shoulder. From time to time Deanie said things that needed no response.

"One time," she said, "when we were real little, Clara and I got dolls alike for Christmas and I broke mine and I dressed it up in Clara's doll's clothes, and she thought her doll was broken. I never did tell anybody and I still have the doll. It's perfect."

"There, there," Delores said. Deanie's tears ran unnoticed onto Delores's blouse, turning it a darker color.

"And one time we were going to play piano pieces for our grandmother, and Clara only knew one piece. It was 'The Spinning Song,' and I begged to go first and then I played her piece and she didn't have anything to play! I don't know why I did that."

Deanie's father was dialing. "Hilton? Has Frances Malcolm come back yet?"

On the sofa Deanie looked at her father and said, "I want to talk to her too."

He nodded without glancing around. "Well, would you have her call this number when she gets in?"

There was a silence after he hung up the telephone, and then Deanie's voice, saying, "And one time—this was when we were real little—I . . ."

John D let the picture of the room, and the words, fade away. He concentrated on the harbor. The boats were being tied up. Fishermen were clomping up the walkway with their catch. Shipowners were readying their ships for a possible storm.

Overhead the sky was empty of birds. Gulls and an occasional pelican sat on the pilings, still as statues, facing into the wind.

". . . I don't know why I did things like that." Deanie's voice rose. "Clara was just so easy to trick. I mean, she believed in people and she—"

John D watched a boat pull up to the dock. It was an old boat, and the bare wood showed through the peeling paint. John D could barely make out the name *Seaswept* on its side.

But there was something about the group on the deck that held John D's attention. They weren't just fishermen coming in after a long day. There was an urgency about their movements. Someone's hurt, John D thought.

He watched as two men helped a girl onto the dock. She was wrapped in a blanket. Her legs were bare. There was a towel over her head. She was clutching it under her chin like a kerchief.

With the help of the men, the girl began to walk. She was unsteady, as if she had been at sea a long time.

John D pressed his face closer to the window. His nose touched the glass. He took off his thick eyeglasses and peered through the salt-sprayed window. He could see from a distance better that way.

He watched the girl's slow difficult steps with increasing interest. He felt as if he had stopped breathing.

And then he felt his lungs fill with enough air to burst them. His hands pressed against the glass. The girl lifted her head, the wind caught the towel and blew it down to her shoulders.

Tears filled John D's eyes and goose bumps rose on his thin arms.

"Here's Clara!" he cried.

Everyone was silent as they drove home. They were worn out, drained of emotion. Clara felt she had used her last bit of strength talking to her mother on the telephone.

"Mom, hi, it's me, Clara."

"Hi, I just got in from a meeting and I have two seconds to dress for a banquet. What's wrong?"

Clara could imagine her mother zipping up her new beige dress as she handled the phone, slipping her coral and seashell necklace over her head, checking the result in the mirror.

"Nothing, I'm all right."

"Something must have happened or you wouldn't be calling. Is Deanie all right?"

"We're all fine. I just wanted to let you know— Oh, never mind. Here's Dad."

Her father's voice, deep and calm again, told the story of Clara's being swept out to sea as if he were recapping a game. "Oh, I guess we should have waited, but we wanted to call— Hey, remember that time you let Deanie phone me in the middle of the Steeler game to tell me she almost went through the windshield?" He laughed. "Well, now we're even." He laughed again, then said, "Your mom wants to speak to you again."

Clara had taken the phone. "No, I'm all right. Really, Mom, I'm fine."

"You're sure?"

"My back's sunburned and my eyes sting and I've got water in my ears, but other than that, I'm fine."

She had felt foolish listing the little complaints, but they were like proofs that she was still alive. She could almost feel the sympathy coming through the telephone wire from her mother.

"You take care of yourself."

"I will."

"I miss you."

"I miss you too."

Clara closed her eyes. "You all right?" her father asked, patting her leg. She nodded.

She was, for the first time that she could remember, sitting in the front seat of the car with her father. But she didn't want any more attention. She had had enough—Deanie sobbing, saying, "I'm never going to be mean to you again"; her father picking her up and swinging her around as if she were a child; Delores, tears in her eyes, patting her and saying, "I should never have let you go." Only John D, standing apart and watching with his cool pale eyes, seemed normal.

"I cannot wait to get out of this bathing suit," Deanie said in the backseat. "I feel like I have been living in it for a hundred years."

Clara answered, "Same here," without opening her eyes.

It was true. She felt as if she had been away long enough to travel around the world. She felt as if she had returned from one of those seven-year voyages old sailors used to make. She imagined the homecoming. "It's so good to see you. It's grand to have you home at last." And then the silence, as everyone realized that in seven years the old sailor had become an absolute stranger.

"What are you thinking about?" her father asked.

It was the first time anyone had ever been interested in her thoughts. Perhaps a sea voyage made a person more fascinating. She smiled to herself.

"Old sailors."

"What about old sailors?"

"Oh, just that they used to go off on those long, long voyages, and then they would come home and everybody would meet them at the dock and say, 'It's so good to have you home' and everything, and the kids would climb all over them and then everybody would suddenly stop. Because they would realize, you know, that this person was an absolute total stranger."

"Is that how you feel, Clara, like an absolute total stranger?"

"No, I just feel kind of different."

"Better different or worse?"

"Oh, better. I don't know how to explain it, but when you think you're going to die—and when I fell off the float, that's exactly what I thought—'I am going to die.'"

She paused. "Well, when you think you're going to die and you don't! You feel like everything is perfect. The little things don't matter. Tomorrow I'll probably wish I didn't snort like a horse, but tonight I'm just so glad to be here. Everybody ought to almost die at least once."

"I hope I've already had my time. When I was seven Arnie Dalton's little brother hit me over the head with a two-by-four."

Clara laughed.

"What are you two laughing about up there?" Deanie asked, leaning forward. "I cannot hear one single word stuck back here in the backseat."

Clara smiled over her shoulder. "I know," she said.

Clara lay in bed, staring up at the ceiling. The bed still rocked occasionally with the slow, up-and-down movements of the waves. She found herself holding onto the sides.

"How about some soup?" Delores asked from the doorway. Clara shook her head and Delores smiled. "I know you are worn out with being offered food, but we're so glad to have you back that we want to do something for you. You hardly ate any shrimp."

"I'm not hungry."

"Even John D, who never does anything for anybody, volunteered to make you a milk shake."

Clara shook her head.

"Well, call if you want *anything*."

"I will."

Delores went back into the living room. Clara watched

the shadows on the ceiling, the faint light from the lighthouse. She listened to the distant pounding of the surf. The threat of a storm had passed, but the surf was still high and boomed against the shore.

She closed her eyes. When Clara was little, she had had wonderful dreams about disasters. When a tornado was in the news, she dreamed of being whisked away to a land of little people. When a volcano erupted, she dreamed of going to the center of the earth. It was the way everyone wanted to get away, she imagined, off to something different and interesting and exciting. In reality—

"Are you all right? Tell me the truth," Deanie asked.

Clara opened her eyes. "Yes."

Deanie came into the room and sat on the bed. "Weren't you terrified?" she asked, crossing her legs yoga-style.

"Yes."

"I would have died. I really don't believe I could have held on all that time. I would have been *so* scared."

"You would have held on."

"I don't know. I'm not like you. I panic. I remember I was in the pool one time with Marcia's brother—he thinks he's so funny—and he was pulling us under by our legs, and I was just desperate. I was like our cat. Remember when Moonie fell in the pool? I was like

Moonie." She made a cat face and some hand movements under her chin. Then she sat up straighter and said, "Didn't you worry about sharks?"

"No."

"That's all I would have thought about."

"After a while you don't even think."

"Anyway, when you go back to school this fall and Yogurt McCalley asks you to write a theme about something that happened on your vacation, you'll have something to write."

"Teachers don't do that anymore."

" 'My Sea Adventure,' by Clara."

Clara shook her head. "It wasn't like that."

"What?"

"An adventure. You make it sound like getting on the wrong bus or something."

"No, that's what an adventure is—being in danger and getting saved."

Clara sighed. "It wasn't like that."

"Anyway, you would not believe how sickening John D was after you got swept out to sea. He said to me, 'You should have kept an eye on her,' like you were a baby! And then he said, 'Your sister was in a very miserable state of mind.' "

"He said that?"

"Yes, he made it sound like you *let* yourself be swept

146

away. I wanted to throw sand in his eyes. He brings out the two-year-old in me."

"I didn't *let* it happen."

"Of course not."

Still, it seemed to Clara that everything was somehow tied together. She closed her eyes. Life wasn't a series of unrelated things, one event after another, like television. It joined together. It overlapped. And what happened in one hour, one day, affected what happened the next.

"Don't go to sleep," Deanie said, "because I have something important to tell you. This is why I came in. It is up to you whether we go home or not."

"What?"

"It's up to you whether we go home or finish out the two weeks."

"Who says?"

"Dad *and* Delores. They don't want you to be permanently scarred. So when they ask you, say you want to go home. Look, I have already started to peel. I want people to see me before I look like a pinto bean."

"I don't know whether I want to go right home," Clara said slowly.

"Clara, that's stupid!" Deanie struck her fists on the bed.

"It isn't."

"It's like going on the Space Cyclone and making

yourself sick. It's stupid, stupid, stupid!" Grains of sand flew up from the bedspread as Deanie struck it three more times.

"It isn't the same at all."

"Well, would you explain it to me? I thought you would be delighted to go home. I thought you would leap up and start packing."

"I can't explain it," Clara said. "It's just that if I go home now, well, it's like I'm running away."

"But, Clara, you always run away! It wouldn't be you if you didn't run away."

"But this time I'm not. I don't want to go home with this as The Terrible Thing That Broke Up the Vacation."

"It *was* terrible—"

"But it won't be *as* terrible if I stay."

"That makes no sense to me at all." Deanie stood up. "If you want to go home, you should go home. That's what I'd do."

She paused in the lamplight, watching to see if Clara was going to change her mind. "You know what we're going to do if we stay, don't you? Tomorrow we're going crabbing. And tomorrow night we're going on some sort of patrol to watch sea turtles laying eggs on the beach." She waited, then sighed. "Well, I'll go tell the others the wonderful news."

Deanie went into the living room. "I bring you Clara's decision," she announced. "She wants to stay."

"Good," someone answered.

It sounded to Clara like John D's voice, but she did not think that was possible. She was mixed up in a lot of ways about John D. She could not imagine him being the one to discover her missing. She could not imagine him saying, "Clara was in a very miserable state of mind." And what was the other thing he had said to Deanie? "You should have kept an eye on her." She smiled. She felt as strange as if the President or the Pope had noticed her.

"Now, Deanie, you didn't pressure her to stay, did you?" her father asked in the living room.

"I pressured her to go! Look at these arms! I want to get home before I'm a complete eyesore."

"You've got time to get another tan," Delores said.

Clara closed her eyes. The bed was no longer rising and falling like the sea. The sound of the surf no longer beat in her brain. Her fingers relaxed their grip on the sides of the bed.

"I think I'll see if Clara would like some hot tea," Delores said. She smiled. "I know I am being ridiculous, but as the only mother present, I—"

"I'll do it," John D said. He got quickly to his feet.

"Thank you, John D."

149

John D went and stood in the doorway and looked at Clara with his pale eyes. She was back, safe and unharmed, shaken—and yet somehow she seemed more secure. He, on the other hand, was not. His emotions, new and crude and oversize as the beginning of a carving, made a lump in his chest.

He could have written a chapter about it, he thought. "Ways to Avoid Misery." And the first rule would be "Don't care about anybody." But for some reason his book no longer seemed important. He doubted he would finish it.

He put his hands in his pockets, cleared his throat, and said, "Clara, Mom wants to know if you'd like some hot tea."

There was no answer.

"Clara?"

He hesitated to make sure she was asleep. "Well, I'll see you tomorrow," he said, as if he were making a date. Then, with an embarrassed smile to the empty hall, he returned to the living room.

"Clara's asleep," he said.

ABOUT THE AUTHOR

Betsy Byars's sharp perceptions and humor have made her one of America's most popular and honored writers for young people. *The Summer of the Swans* won the Newbery Award in 1971, and in 1981 *The Night Swimmers*, published by Delacorte Press, received the American Book Award for juvenile fiction. It was also a *Boston Globe–Horn Book* Honor Book and a *School Library Journal* Best Book.

Ms. Byars lives in Clemson, South Carolina.